Chains of Love

Juliet reached behind her neck to unfasten the chain.

To her surprise, she couldn't locate the clasp.

Exasperated, she went to the mirror and pulled the chain around, planning to unfasten it from the front.

She stared in the mirror in disbelief; a cold chill rippled over her shoulders.

The clasp was gone!

Juliet turned the chain around and around, unable to believe her eyes. She was certain there had been a clasp when she had put it on. Now, it seemed to have vanished.

Fighting down a wave of fear, Juliet tried one more time to slip the chain over her head.

It was impossible.

"It won't come off," she whispered, her voice tight and small. *"It won't come off!"*

Juliet Dove, Queen of Love

Juliet Dove, Queen of Love

A MAGIC SHOP BOOK

Bruce Coville

MAGIC CARPET BOOKS

HARCOURT, INC.

ORLANDO   AUSTIN   NEW YORK   SAN DIEGO   TORONTO   LONDON

Requests for permission to make copies of any part of
the work should be mailed to the following address:
Permissions Department, Harcourt, Inc.,
6277 Sea Harbor Drive, Orlando, Florida 32887-6777.

www.HarcourtBooks.com

First Magic Carpet Books edition 2005

Magic Carpet Books is a trademark of Harcourt, Inc., registered in
the United States of America and/or other jurisdictions.

The Library of Congress has cataloged
the hardcover edition as follows:
Coville, Bruce.
Juliet Dove, Queen of Love/Bruce Coville.
p.   cm.
"A Magic Shop Book."
Summary: A shy twelve-year-old girl must solve a puzzle
involving characters from Greek mythology to free herself
from a spell which makes her irresistible to boys.
[1. Magic—Fiction.   2. Bashfulness—Fiction.
3. Mythology, Greek—Fiction.]   I. Title.
PZ7.C8344Ju   2003
[Fic]—dc22   2003011846
ISBN 0-15-204561-9
ISBN 0-15-205217-8 pb

Text set in New Baskerville
Designed by Lydia D'moch

A C E G H F D B
Printed in the United States of America

for Tamora Pierce

*(with a special note of thanks
to Cara for the sluggarium)*

Contents

Juliet Dove, Queen of Love

ONE

Killer Strikes Again

"Hey, Killer! How's your boyfriend?"

Juliet Dove felt her cheeks begin to burn. Why couldn't Bambi Quilp just leave her alone? Why couldn't *everyone* just leave her alone?

"I don't have a boyfriend," she said softly.

"Oh, we've seen you walking with Arturo," said Bambi knowingly.

"Yeah, we've seen you walking with Arturo!" repeated Samantha Foster, who was sort of Bambi's official leech.

That Bambi and Samantha had seen Juliet and Arturo walking together was no surprise. Arturo Perez was Juliet's across-the-backyard neighbor, and they had been walking to school together since first grade.

"Artureo and Juliet, the love story of the century!" cried Bambi. Clasping her hands she placed them against her cheek and fluttered her eyelids. "How Juliet does luh-uve that may-unn!"

Juliet flared. "Look who's talking, you pea-brained, metal-mouthed boy chaser! Did you ever see anything in pants that you didn't want? You'll probably have to wait to get the tin off your teeth, though. I hear boys don't like the taste of stainless steel!"

Juliet knew she'd made a mistake the moment the words left her mouth. Bambi had only been wearing braces since Monday and she was still sensitive about them. But Juliet had been desperate to turn the attention away from herself, and the blistering comments had escaped her lips before she even had a chance to think about them.

Explosions like this were what had earned her the ridiculous nickname Killer to begin with—ridiculous because, in truth, Juliet was the most painfully shy person in the entire Venus Harbor Middle School. Or the entire state, by her father's calculation. But Mr. Dove was given to poetic exaggeration.

Juliet hated the nickname, especially because the ferocious comments that earned it for her had never been spoken out of anger. It was just that the minute people started teasing her about personal matters, she felt such an acute panic that she would say anything—*anything*—to get them to leave her alone. Unfortunately, whenever she tried to explain that she did this because she was shy, people laughed.

"It's because you're too good at it," Arturo had told her once. "I mean, when you set your tongue on slice and dice, it's like you've got a Ginsu knife between your teeth."

Juliet might not have lashed out at Bambi quite so horribly if she hadn't already been upset over their language-arts teacher's announcement that they would be doing oral reports at the end of the month. As far as Juliet was concerned, doing an oral report was not much different from being slowly ground up in a sausage machine—except that, given a choice, she would have opted for the sausage machine. She could not think of anything more excruciating than having to stand up in front of people and speak.

All this was going through Juliet's mind later that afternoon as she pressed herself against the brick wall of the alley that ran alongside the Venus Harbor Cinema. She had ducked around the corner to hide when she saw Bambi and Samantha coming toward her. Though she kept telling herself that the simplest way to deal with the situation would be to walk up to Bambi and apologize, Juliet found the very idea terrifying. So she remained tight against the wall, barely breathing, wishing she could melt right into it, until the girls had gone by.

Unfortunately, Bambi and Samantha—Did either of them ever go anywhere alone? Juliet wondered—did not keep walking. Instead, they stopped to examine the poster for the weekend's big event, the Third Annual Venus Harbor Valentine's Day Poetry Jam.

Go away, thought Juliet desperately. *Go away!*

The mental command didn't work. Bambi and Samantha stayed right where they were.

"My pathetic mother is totally jazzed because Scott Willis is coming to this," said Bambi.

"Who cares about a fat weatherman?" scoffed Samantha. "Corey Falcon is the one I'm excited about!"

"Just because you've got fifteen pictures of him on your wall?"

"You think he's hot, too!" protested Samantha.

"Besides, did you ever read any of his poems? He's not just a great actor. He's got a beautiful soul!"

Juliet tried not to betray her hiding spot by making puking noises. The whole poetry jam was her father's idea and he had been grumbling for months about having to bring in "fake poets" like Scott Willis and Corey Falcon. She felt a twitch of irritation at Bambi and Samantha for even looking at the poster.

"So are you going to go?" asked Samantha, after a few minutes.

"Are you kidding?" said Bambi. "And miss a chance to see Corey Falcon in person? Besides, it's going to be fun. People are coming from all over. They even did a thing about it on Fox News last night." Suddenly she laughed.

"What's so funny?" asked Samantha.

"Remember what happened to Juliet the first year they did this?"

Samantha snorted. "That was so pathetic!"

Juliet's cheeks blazed nearly as red as the brick wall behind her as the unwanted memory swept over her. More than ever she wished she could just disappear.

"So—what are you going to do about her?" asked Samantha.

"About who?" said Bambi, sounding genuinely puzzled.

"Juliet!"

"Why should I do anything? Everyone knows what a jerk she is. I've got more important things to do than worry about getting back at Killer."

"I can't believe you're going to let her get away with saying those things," growled Samantha. "In fact, when I see her, I'm going to slap her face *for* you!"

A horrible panic, too powerful to resist, seized Juliet, and she turned to flee. She did not run because she was afraid of being slapped by Samantha. She ran simply because she was afraid of being seen by either of them.

The back end of the alley opened into the parking lot behind Cosgrove's grocery. Juliet raced across the lot, ignoring the hello called to her by Suzy Cosgrove. She shot behind the teddy-bear store, turned up Dell Street, then turned right, toward the beach. But somehow she must have gotten turned around, because the beach was only two blocks away, and she kept running and running. To her surprise, she found herself on a street she did not recognize—which seemed impossible, since she had lived in Venus Harbor all her life, and it wasn't that big a town.

Juliet slowed to a walk, pressing her hand against her side where a sharp pain had blossomed. She noticed that a mist had started to rise. Early fogs were not unknown in Venus Harbor, but this was thicker than usual, and the tendrils of it seemed to cling to her feet. She pulled her drab sweater more tightly around her shoulders and looked from side to side.

The street was lined with old-fashioned–looking shops. Like the fog, this was not unusual for Venus Harbor, where quaint was the official town style and nine-tenths of the stores—half of them selling either fudge or seashells—were designed to catch the eye of tourists. But the shop at the end of the street was even more old-fashioned–looking than the others. Its curved front window, divided into many panes, said in bold letters:

ELIVES' MAGIC SUPPLIES
S. H. ELIVES, PROP.

Where did that *come from?* wondered Juliet, finding it hard to believe Venus Harbor could possibly contain such a cool store—or that she had been unaware of it until now. Forgetting Bambi and Samantha, she waded through the fog, which was swirling around her knees now and seemed to get thicker as she approached the shop.

The door was made of carved wood instead of metal and glass like those of most of the stores in town. Juliet pressed on it.

The door swung open without a sound. A small bell tinkled overhead as she crossed the threshold.

She looked around for a clerk but there was no one in sight.

"Hello?" she called. "Anyone here?"

No answer.

Juliet thought about leaving but figured if the door was unlocked it must mean the store was open for business. Maybe whoever ran the place was in the bathroom. Juliet actually preferred it like this, since she wouldn't have to talk to anyone. She hated the way people who worked in stores were always asking if you wanted something; most of the time what she wanted was to be left alone.

She gazed around the shop. It was filled with all sorts of things that magicians—*professional* magicians—might use in their acts. To the right was a wall filled with cages. She saw rabbits, which she figured were for pulling out of hats. But there were also toads, lizards, bats, and a spider the size of a dinner plate. She shuddered, and turned her attention elsewhere.

In the center of the room stood a tall, glossy black cabinet with brilliantly colored Asian dragons painted on its sides. Swords had been thrust through the cabinet from all directions.

Beside the cabinet was a bin filled with a rainbow's worth of silk scarves.

A glass-topped counter ran against the wall to the left, its shelves filled with Chinese rings, big decks of cards, and other magician's paraphernalia. On top of the counter was a rack of magic wands.

At the back of the shop was another counter. This one, made of wood, had a dragon carved on its front. On top of the counter sat an old-fashioned brass cash register. Juliet thought it was quite beautiful, but she was even more impressed by the stuffed owl perched on top of it. At least she assumed the owl was stuffed, until it turned its head, looked right at her, blinked twice, then uttered a low hoot.

"Peace, Uwila!" cried a sharp voice from the back of the shop. "I know she's there."

The owl looked startled.

A moment later a woman strode through the beaded curtain that covered the door behind the counter. She was attractive, or would have been if not for a leanness in her features that made what beauty she had seem harsh and forbidding. She wore black pants, a high-necked white blouse, and a long overshirt made of red fabric and covered in designs so sharp and pointed they seemed to jab your eyes.

Juliet wondered if she was the owner of the shop. If so, was she Mrs. Elives, Miss Elives, or Ms. Elives? She hated trying to figure out what to call an adult woman. Why couldn't it be as simple as it was for men, where there was just one choice?

The owl swiveled its head toward the woman, then ruffled its feathers and hooted questioningly.

"Peace, Uwila!" said the woman again.

The owl returned to its motionless state. Juliet could not help but notice that its eyes seemed to be filled with terror. She felt a surge of anger. Did this woman mistreat the poor thing? How could you have something as wonderful as an owl for a pet and be cruel to it?

"Welcome," said the woman. Her voice was dry and husky, as if she had not used it in some time. "My name is... Iris. How can I help you?"

Juliet stared at her for a moment before she was able to say, "I just came in to look around. I hadn't seen the store before. I thought I knew all the shops in town."

The woman smiled. "We're a little off the beaten path." She paused, stared at Juliet for a moment, then nodded in satisfaction. "Let me show you something." Reaching into the pocket of her overshirt, she extracted a gold chain from which hung a small, delicately carved pendant—ivory, by the look of it.

"Cupid's choice," murmured the woman, her voice suddenly softer and more enticing than Juliet would have thought possible. "Here, take a closer look. Hold it for a moment!"

When Juliet took a step forward, the woman grabbed her hand, pulled it toward her, and dropped the pendant into it.

Startled by the sudden action, Juliet nearly turned to run out of the shop. But she was too fascinated to leave. Lifting the pendant so she could examine it more closely, she felt her heart captured by the strangely beautiful face carved into the ivory, found herself filled with a desire to own it. She noticed a tiny pair of golden hinges on one side and a miniature keyhole, also made of gold, on the other. Her fingers moved toward them.

"Don't!" said the woman urgently. Lowering her voice she added, "Not that you could. The hinges don't work. Still, best not to try. You might ruin everything."

Juliet looked at the woman nervously. She was talking as if she were crazy. Juliet was tempted to drop the pendant and flee. But the thing was so lovely, she couldn't help looking at it again. She couldn't remember ever wanting an object so desperately.

"How much is it?" she asked, knowing full well that she could never afford such an exquisite item.

"How badly do you want it?" countered the woman.

"Not much," replied Juliet. This was not true. However, Juliet didn't consider it a lie; her father had taught her about bargaining, and this was just part of the process. You never let someone know how much you wanted something.

The woman laughed. "Fine. Just put it down and leave."

Juliet did place the pendant on the counter. But she found that, somehow, she couldn't bring herself to let go of it.

"How badly do you want it?" asked the woman again. Her face was tighter now, her eyes as steely gray as the ocean in midwinter.

"Where did it come from?" asked Juliet, partly to gain time to think, partly because she was frightened. "Who made it?"

The woman stared directly into her eyes. "It is the key to the world's desire."

Juliet forced herself to open her fingers and let go of the pendant. She turned to go but had not walked more than three steps toward the door before she turned back. Though she was frightened by her desire for the object, she had to know more. Putting her hands firmly on either side of the ivory bauble, but refusing to allow herself to actually touch it, she asked again, "How much is it?"

"It's not for sale," said the woman, smiling for the first time.

Juliet stared at her, puzzled. What kind of gimmick was this?

The woman's face grew solemn. "It's not for sale," she repeated. "Even so, if you want it enough, you can have it. But you must want it, Juliet, *really* want it. Otherwise it's no deal."

Juliet looked up at the woman. "How do you know my name?"

"That's not the real question right now. The question is, how much do you want this amulet?"

"I don't understand."

The woman shrugged. "No one does. That's part of what makes life so interesting." She gestured toward the chain. "Go ahead, pick it up again."

Juliet hesitated, then reached for the amulet. To her surprise, she was not able to lift it off the counter. She felt a ripple of fear. What was going on here?

The woman shrugged again, looking disappointed. "I guess you don't want it badly enough after all." She put her own hand over the amulet and began to slide it toward her.

"Wait!" cried Juliet.

The woman stopped, lifted her hand.

Juliet reached out again. The amulet felt warm beneath her fingers. Suddenly a powerful longing swept over her, a strange and passionate need to possess it. She closed her hand over the ivory bauble and, without the slightest effort, scooped it up.

The owl hooted ominously and ruffled its feathers. A gust of wind battered the shop windows.

The woman, on the other hand, looked pleased. Giving Juliet a dazzling smile, she said, "I thought you might be the one. I was hoping—" She stopped and glanced over her shoulder, as if she had heard a sound, then turned back to Juliet. "You should go! Take the side door, it will get you home more quickly. Go. Go *now!*"

Terrified by the change in the woman's tone, Juliet turned. But before she could leave, the woman cried, "Wait!"

Juliet turned back. The woman's eyes were blazing.

"Speak of this to no one!" she commanded.

Juliet nodded, turned once more, and fled through the side door. To her astonishment, she found herself back in the alley where she had started.

Had she made some sort of big circle when she ran from Bambi and Samantha? She didn't think so—but if not, how had she arrived back here? She glanced around and was relieved to find the two girls nowhere in sight. She spent no more time thinking about them, for something stronger and stranger and more frightening was occupying her mind.

It was what she had seen when she glanced back before leaving the shop. The woman behind the counter had been smiling—a fierce, eager smile. And her eyes had been lit with a look that was both hungry and triumphant.

The very memory of it made Juliet shudder.

She opened her hand to stare at the amulet again. Extending the forefinger of her left hand, she touched the beautifully carved ivory. A jolt of power, almost like an electric shock, stung her. Juliet stared at the amulet in awe, then crammed it into her pocket and ran for home.

TWO

Spring Fever

The Doves lived eight blocks from the shore, in a rambling old house they'd inherited from Mr. Dove's great aunt Bessie, who had owned one of the town's first gift shops. Juliet had never met Great Aunt Bessie. Even so, she felt almost as if she knew the old woman—partly because she had spent a lot of time in the attic poring over albums filled with photographs from Bessie's life, partly because her father had told them so many stories about Bessie, whom he always described as having "the face of an angel and the heart of a pirate."

Mr. Dove tended to speak this way. He taught poetry at the state university, about forty miles away, and loved words with, as he put it, "a passion that passeth understanding." Mr. Dove—or Prof, as he was known to the neighbors—was the one who had convinced the Venus Harbor town council to have an annual poetry jam on Valentine's Day, on the theory that the town ought to take more advantage of being named for the goddess of love.

Juliet would have thought this was quite wonderful—she loved poetry—were it not for the fact that her father wanted her to participate in this year's jam, even after what had happened the first year. In Juliet's opinion, this was like saying, "Hey, honey, why don't you take off your shoes and walk barefoot over hot coals. It'll be fun!"

It wasn't that she didn't have poems in her head; each of the Dove children was expected to memorize at least one poem a month. It was just that death held less terror for her than standing in front of a crowd to speak.

As Juliet drew near the house, her hand still clutching the mysterious amulet in her pocket, she could see by the cars in the driveway that her parents were both home. A third car, unfamiliar to Juliet, indicated her mother had probably invited someone from the library for dinner. Mrs. Dove volunteered at the Venus Harbor Free Library two afternoons a week, and she loved bringing other workers home with her. Though this was very kind, it was a habit that made life hard for any shy people who happened to be living in the house. Not that any of the Doves other than Juliet had an ounce of shyness in them.

Juliet slipped through the back door, hoping to come in without being noticed.

No such luck.

"You're late!" called Mrs. Dove from the living room, her voice cheerful. "Wash up and hurry on in. Supper's almost ready, and we've got company."

Juliet sighed. Trudging upstairs, she went to her room and dumped her books on her bed. Then in the bathroom she ran a little water over her hands— a gesture she knew her mother would never really consider washing.

"Ah, here she is at last!" cried Margaret, when Juliet came thumping into the living room.

Margaret was Juliet's big sister. She was also a big tease, which could be amusing but was mostly annoying. Now that she was seventeen, she liked to associate with the adults. Their younger siblings, Byron and Clarice, still preferred to associate with the television set and were undoubtedly in the family room doing just that.

Juliet noticed that Margaret's hair, which was only about an inch long, was blue.

She was pretty sure it had been green the day before.

The Dove family had a hard time keeping track of Margaret's hair colors.

Sitting on the love seat was a striking-looking woman whom Juliet had never met. The woman had a high forehead, a prominent nose, and warm, friendly eyes. She was beautiful, but not like a Hollywood actress. It was a much more interesting kind of beautiful.

"Juliet, I'd like you to meet Hyacinth Priest," said her mother. "She's in town for a few weeks to teach a storytelling class at the library."

"She's also going to be one of the judges for the poetry jam," said Mr. Dove.

"I'm very pleased to make your acquaintance," said Juliet, repeating the phrase her mother had drilled into her. She stepped dutifully forward to shake Ms. Priest's hand.

The woman stood. She wore a flowing dress patterned with swirls of color—more colors than Juliet could count—and a pair of earrings from which dangled moons and stars. Taking Juliet's hand in hers, she said, "And I am very pleased to meet *you*, Juliet Dove." Her voice was warm, and she spoke with great precision.

Juliet started to back away, but Ms. Priest tightened her grip. Lowering her voice, she said intensely, "I expect we will get to know each other very well in the days to come, Juliet."

Juliet blinked in surprise, but Ms. Priest dropped her hand and sat back down, as if she had not said something extraordinary at all.

A buzzer sounded from the kitchen. "Dinner's ready!" cried Mrs. Dove brightly. "Juliet, go get the little ones, would you?"

She was glad for an excuse to escape the room.

Dinner was excellent, if a little exotic for Juliet's taste. Mr. and Mrs. Dove were both good cooks, and they liked to work together in the kitchen, where they took an unfortunate delight in trying new recipes from "authentic ethnic cuisines."

The young Doves were expected to eat this stuff, no matter how strange it might seem. Fortunately, there were some limits. Three years earlier, the children—led by Margaret—had negotiated a compromise that allowed their parents to try new recipes twice a week as long as they never served liver, brussels sprouts, or any meat that came from an animal you might be able to buy in a pet store. (This last item had been added to the list the day Margaret caught Mr. Dove studying a book on the cuisine of South America, including complete instructions on how to cook a guinea pig.)

Clarice had found her own way around the dinner problem. At the age of two—she was now four—she had introduced the family to her new best friend, Mr. Toe. Now Mr. Toe joined them for dinner every night. His place was marked by a saucer set next to Clarice's own plate—a saucer where she carefully piled small amounts of food for him to eat. Juliet had noticed that Clarice mostly fed Mr. Toe whatever it was that she did not like herself. Juliet had also noticed that it didn't seem to bother Clarice that Mr. Toe never actually ate any of it.

Once Juliet asked Clarice what Mr. Toe looked like.

"He's a toe, silly," she had replied, sounding a little miffed.

"Pinky?" asked Juliet, genuinely curious.

Clarice shook her head. "Big," she said firmly. "He's about this tall," she added, holding her hand a foot above the floor.

"Does he have eyes?" Juliet had persisted.

"Go away," was all Clarice would say.

Juliet still had not decided how she felt about her little sister having a giant big toe for a best friend.

Sometimes she was amused by the idea. Other times she found it flat out embarrassing.

Despite the presence of a stranger, Juliet actually had a good time at supper. Her mother had once pointed out, when Juliet was complaining about how often Mrs. Dove brought people home, that Juliet almost *always* had a good time after she got over her initial shyness. Juliet had to admit this was true. However, she was not convinced it made up for the half hour or so of intense discomfort she always suffered first.

Her father was in fine form, quoting poetry right and left. Before Mrs. Dove brought in the main course, he rose and said, "The actual occasion for tonight's dinner is to bid farewell to our kitchen floor, which Margaret and I are about to replace in response to many years of requests from her mother, my beloved spousal unit. Therefore, I propose a toast to the floor that was, which we shall miss but shall not mourn."

Lifting his glass, he said,

"Farewell, floor,
 You've served us well,
 But now you're old and cracking.
 It's time, make way
 For younger tiles
 That have the glow you're lacking!"

Then they all raised their glasses—the adults with wine, the children with milk or water—in farewell to the floor. Not long after that, Ms. Priest told a story that was so funny it made Byron spit milk through his nose.

So all in all it was a lovely evening.

While the adults were having coffee, Juliet excused herself. "I'm going to Arturo's," she whispered to her mother.

This was expected. Juliet and Arturo had been doing their homework together since first grade.

"Don't be late, dear," said Mrs. Dove. The words were spoken more as a ritual than anything else; Arturo's mother never allowed them to work too late.

As Juliet crossed the backyard, heading for the gap in the hedge that would let her pass from their lawn to that of the Perez family, she stopped to admire the tall green shoots thrusting up from the tulip bulbs she had helped her mother plant the previous fall. The buds on some of them were swelling, almost ready to burst. She couldn't wait to see them.

Arturo was at the kitchen table, books out and ready to work. He was a handsome boy—not that Juliet ever thought of him that way—with thick black hair and a snub of a nose. His dark eyes were framed by extraordinarily long lashes.

Since they were working at Arturo's house, they started with spelling, which was his specialty.

The first word on the list was *amorous.*

"Amorous," said Juliet. "A-M-O-U-R—"

"Wrong!" cried Arturo, a little too gleefully.

Juliet rolled her eyes and tried again. "Amorous.

A-M-O-R-O-U-S. Amorous. What the heck does it mean, anyway?"

"Romantic, or filled with desire," said Arturo, who sometimes reminded her of a small version of her father. "It's from the Latin root *amo,* which means 'to love.'"

"All right, all right!" said Juliet, who didn't like to talk about this kind of thing. "Let's get back to the list."

She was relieved when they finally finished their spelling and could move on to math, which was *her* specialty.

Opening their books, they started working on a series of word problems that involved figuring out how much profit a store could make on cream of mushroom soup. Sometime after the third problem, Juliet noticed that Arturo didn't seem to be concentrating on the math. Instead, he kept glancing at her, then looking down whenever she looked back at him.

"What *is* it?" she snapped at last. "Do I have spinach in my teeth or something?"

Arturo shook his head. "No, it's just that . . . well, I never noticed how pretty your hair is before."

Juliet looked at him in astonishment. "What did you say?"

Arturo's eyes widened, and he couldn't have looked more surprised if he had just discovered that he had laid an egg. "Nothing," he said quickly. "Forget it."

Juliet squinted at him for a second, then turned back to the math work. But she couldn't help glancing up at him every now and then. He kept staring at her. Finally she slammed her book shut and snapped, "Will you keep your eyes to yourself?"

"I'm trying to," Arturo said, sounding miserable. "But they won't do what I tell them!"

"That is the most pathetic thing I have ever heard in my life!" said Juliet. "You're going to have to do better than that if you want to get anywhere with girls."

"Who said I want to get anywhere with girls?"

"Well, why are you looking at me that way?"

"I don't know!"

"That's it," said Juliet. "You can just keep your X-ray eyes to yourself. I'm out of here!"

Scooping up her books, she sailed through the kitchen, barely nodding to Mrs. Perez, who was sitting in the living room watching a *telenovela*.

Juliet stalked out into a night that was lashed by a crisp wind. The sea air, even eight blocks inland, was delicious. She gazed up at the sky. The moon, growing toward fullness, seemed to be floating on a bed of clouds that glowed silver with its light. Other clouds drifted in front of the moon like veils, shifting and moving so that she could never quite see all of it. It made her think of Arturo and his furtive glances. *What the heck was that all about?* she wondered uncomfortably.

Juliet had just stepped through the gap in the hedge when she caught the scent of flowers in bloom.

She looked down and almost dropped her books. The tulip buds she had noticed earlier that evening were now wide open. Juliet furrowed her brow. Her mother had showed her how tulips bloomed years ago: Their blossoms opened in sunlight and closed when it got dark.

They did *not* open at night.

She noticed a mist creeping about her feet, and shuddered. After what had happened earlier today, the sight of it made her nervous.

Looking up again, Juliet saw a tall woman standing about thirty feet away. The woman was surrounded by mist—too much of it for Juliet to see her clearly. The only thing she could tell for certain was that the woman was dressed all in white. Slowly, in the most graceful movement Juliet had ever seen, she raised an arm, beckoning. Part of Juliet longed to respond. But she stood without moving, her normal shyness magnified a hundredfold by the weirdness of the situation.

The woman beckoned again, more urgently.

Juliet still did not—could not—move.

"Be wise!" called the woman in a voice that sounded as if it came from much farther away than she was standing.

Faint as the words were, Juliet could sense a desperate note in them. But before she could call back to ask what they meant, the mist rose and swirled around the woman, blocking her from view.

Juliet hesitated, uncertain whether to step forward or flee. As she wavered, a sudden gust of wind blew the mist away.

When it was gone, the woman had vanished as well.

THREE

Boy Trouble

Juliet stood gaping at the spot where the woman had been standing. Surely she had not really vanished. She must have slipped away in the mist or something. But who was she? Why was she wearing such a weird outfit? And what the heck did she mean by "Be wise!"?

Trembling, Juliet hurried across the lawn and into the house. Ms. Priest was still there, listening politely as Mr. Dove carried on about the "poetic tradition." Juliet desperately wanted to tell her parents what had happened with Arturo. But she couldn't stand to do it in front of a stranger; it was too private.

"Everything go all right, Juli?" called her mother.

"Fine," mumbled Juliet.

"Speak up, dear," said Mrs. Dove. "I can't hear you."

"And come on in and say good night," added her father.

Shyly, Juliet stepped into the living room. "Good night, everyone," she said, her voice so soft it was almost inaudible. She wanted to get her good-night kisses but was too embarrassed to do so in front of Ms. Priest.

Her father stretched out a hand and said—as he had every night for as long as she could remember—"'Good night, good night! Parting is such sweet sorrow, that I shall say good night till it be morrow.'"

Blushing, and mentally kicking herself for being such a sissy, Juliet trudged up the stairs.

The light was still on in Byron's room, so she went in to tell him good night. He was at his desk, working on a drawing of an airplane surrounded by blazing guns and explosions.

"What do you think?" he asked, moving his arm so she could see it.

"You're getting better. I like the way you made the plane look as if it's coming right at you."

"Mom showed me how to do that," he said happily.

Their mother was a cartoonist, and Byron hoped to follow in her footsteps. The difference was that while Mrs. Dove's drawings were about family life, Byron's were all about war, death, explosions, and violence. The Doves had worried about this until Byron's teacher told them that every third-grade class she had taught for the last twenty years had had at least three boys who drew that kind of thing, and as far as she knew, all but one of them had grown up to be normal, healthy citizens.

Juliet sat and talked with Byron for a while, not about anything in particular, just because she liked being with him.

"I think that Ms. Priest person is pretty cool," he said as he continued to work on his drawing.

Juliet shrugged. "She's okay. I just wish Mom would stop bringing home complete strangers."

"Do you want her to bring home incomplete strangers?" asked Byron with a grin.

Juliet biffed his ear. "Do you have your poem ready?" she asked, by way of changing the subject.

"Sure. I'm way ahead of Dad."

Juliet wasn't surprised. Though the Dove children were only required to learn one new poem every month, she suspected that Byron had enough Shel Silverstein already tucked away in his head to carry him through the next three years—somewhat to the despair of their father, who had been hoping to have his offspring memorize more elevated works. On this matter Mrs. Dove had taken Byron's side, insisting that if the children were required to memorize that many poems, then they should have some choice in what the poems actually were.

Juliet suspected that Mrs. Dove had begun to regret her intervention sometime between Byron's thirtieth and fortieth recitations of "Someone Ate the Baby."

"What about you?" asked Byron. "You going to do a poem at Dad's festival?"

"When rats fly!" said Juliet dismissively, wishing she had never brought up the subject. She tousled Byron's hair, then headed for her own room, stopping first to peer at her little sister. Clarice was sleeping soundly, thumb tucked firmly in her mouth.

Juliet sighed. Sometimes she wished she could be a little kid again. Life was so much simpler then!

As she was getting undressed, she found the amulet in her pocket. She had meant to show it to her mother when she first came home, but everything had been all crazy because they had company. She admired the delicate carving again. Then she opened the tiny clasp, put the chain around her neck, and fastened it.

She felt dizzy for an instant. From somewhere came a sound almost like a sigh.

Juliet shook her head and glanced around.

She was alone. *Alone and imagining things,* she told herself. She grabbed her brush and ran it through her tangled red curls, glancing in the mirror as she did. For once, she was not unhappy with what she saw.

I'm pretty, she thought in surprise.

When Juliet went down to breakfast the next morning, she found her mother making coffee and Margaret standing at the sink, watering her slug.

"How's Smitty today?" asked Juliet.

Smitty was the name of the slug. Margaret had brought him home from the Venus Harbor Floral Emporium (motto: "We let your love bloom!"), where she had a weekend job. She kept Smitty in a glass container she called the sluggarium and fed him flowers from work. He had been less than an inch long when she first found him. Now he was as big as Margaret's pinky finger—which was where he happened to be resting at the moment, happily stretching out his eye stalks as she ran a gentle stream of warm water over his back. Margaret had added three snails and another slug to the container over the last few months, but Smitty—who was named for an ex-boyfriend—was still her favorite. She claimed she preferred slugs because they had the courage to travel without a shell.

Margaret's cat, Queen Baboo de la Roo (usually referred to by Mr. Dove as "that surly pile of fur-covered fat"), was sitting on the counter next to Margaret, watching the entire process with fascination. The cat did not belong there, but Mr. Dove had long since despaired of enforcing that rule.

Every once in a while, Queen Baboo would stretch a tentative paw toward the slug. Fortunately for Smitty, a sharp word from Margaret was enough to make the cat pull back.

Yawning, Juliet went to the table. Her mother had a bowl of cereal already set out for her.

"Good morning, sleepyhead!" said Mrs. Dove cheerfully. Then she stopped what she was doing to stare at Juliet. "You're looking particularly lovely this morning," she said at last.

Juliet felt herself blush. "Thank you," she murmured. Then, taking a deep breath, she said, "Mom, Arturo acted really weird last night."

"Arturo was born weird," said Margaret from her place at the sink.

"At least he doesn't have a pet slug," shot back Juliet.

"He ought to get one," replied Margaret calmly. "Might do him some good to have a brother."

Mrs. Dove sighed. "Acted weird in what way?" she

asked, pouring herself a cup of coffee and coming to sit in front of Juliet.

"I don't know. He kept looking at me."

"That's weird all right," said Margaret.

"And he told me my hair was pretty."

"Weirder and weirder," said Margaret, nodding her head wisely. "Maybe we should call the men in white coats to come and take him away."

"That's not weird, dear," said Mrs. Dove, ignoring her eldest daughter. "Arturo has just started to notice that you're a girl."

"And you don't think that's weird?" asked Margaret, who had transferred Smitty back into the sluggarium and was now bathing one of the snails.

"Margaret, don't you have something else to do?" asked Mrs. Dove.

Margaret shook her head happily. "I'm free as a bird," she trilled.

"Well, if you can't keep out of this, I'll *find* something for you to do," said Mrs. Dove sharply.

Margaret made a face. "Come on, kids," she said, picking up the sluggarium. "I can tell when we're not wanted!"

Mrs. Dove shook her head. "If that girl wasn't such good source material, I might have to do something terrible to her."

Her comic strip, *The Sheldons,* was set underwater. Even so, it featured a family whose antics sometimes veered too close to the Doves' real life for the taste of her children.

"It's all right, Mom," said Juliet. "You can do something terrible to Margaret if you want."

Mrs. Dove sighed. "The fans would never forgive me. Now, let's talk about Arturo. Was he rude to you?"

Juliet thought for a moment. "No, he was just... well, kind of mushy." She made a face at the memory. Then, speaking more slowly, she said, "But that wasn't the only weird thing that happened last night."

Speaking quietly, even though there was no one else in the kitchen, she told her mother about the flowers and the mysterious woman in white. Juliet wanted to tell her mother about the amulet, too. But somehow that was harder to talk about, and before she could figure out how to explain it without sounding totally crazy, Mrs. Dove pushed herself away from the table, saying, "Let's go outside. I want to see the flowers. And I want to take a look at where this woman was standing."

Juliet followed her mother into the backyard. As they walked toward the flower beds, she saw at once that the tulip buds were tightly closed.

"I swear they were open, Mom," said Juliet. She knew she sounded a little desperate now.

"I don't understand how that could be," said Mrs. Dove gently. She cupped one of the buds in her hand. "Look, Juliet. This won't be ready to bloom for days yet." She looked around. "All right, where was this woman standing?"

"Over there."

Together they went to examine the spot where Juliet had seen the white-clad woman. The ground, moist and muddy from recent rains, was marked by small, light footprints.

"How old do you think she was?" asked Mrs. Dove.

"I couldn't tell. I didn't get that close. And it was kind of foggy."

Mrs. Dove sighed. "I suspect it was Nonny Clark's great aunt Alvina. Poor Alvie is a little, well, you know..." Mrs. Dove shrugged and let the words dangle. "Alvie's not supposed to be out on her own, but sometimes she wanders at night."

All the kids in the neighborhood knew about Alvina Clark, of course. They liked to whisper about the crazy things she did—even though only two or three of them had ever actually seen the woman.

Juliet was one of them. Late one night, two summers earlier, she had poked her head out of her window to look at the stars. While she was staring up, she heard a strange voice crooning wordlessly. Looking for it, she spotted an old woman dressed in a white nightgown on the back porch of the Clark house. Like Juliet, Alvina had been staring at the sky. Unlike Juliet, she had had her arms stretched upward, as if she were begging the stars to take her away.

Remembering the moment, which was both beautiful and strange, Juliet said, "I suppose it could have been her." She paused, then asked, "Is she dangerous?"

"Alvina?" Mrs. Dove laughed. "No, dear. Alvie's a real sweetheart. She's just a little odd. I'm sorry if she frightened you."

Juliet followed her mother back into the house. It was a relief to know that the woman she had seen was only the local oddball.

The problem was she couldn't quite convince herself that that was who it really had been.

"As for Arturo," said her mother, when they were back inside, "my advice is to pretend it never happened." She glanced at her watch. "Your dad's got an early class. I'll bet he'd drive you to school if you want."

Normally Juliet would have walked with Arturo. But since she didn't want to see him this morning, she welcomed the offer.

The inside of the car seemed too small to contain Mr. Dove's high spirits. "We're getting a lot of press coverage for the poetry jam, Juliet. Of course, that's mostly because we've got Scott Willis coming. I'm afraid listening to his drivel is going to drive me slightly nuts."

"Then why did you invite him?" asked Juliet.

Mr. Dove shrugged. "I figure it's a small price to pay for all the publicity he's brought us. Besides, if people come to hear him and then get exposed to real poetry—well, who knows how many people we might turn on to the good stuff?"

"Sneaky, Dad," said Juliet with a smile.

"I prefer to think of it as a covert strike for art. And it's working. We've got entrants coming in from five states. Even so, we're still a little weak in the junior division. Sure you don't want to be part of it?"

"Couldn't I just poke sticks in my eyes instead?"

"See? You've got a wonderful gift for expressive language. Why keep it to yourself?"

Juliet turned and stared out the window. She was starting to wish that she had walked to school after all. What made this really hard was that there was nothing in the world she wanted more than to please her father. But she had tried entering the jam two years ago. It was not an experience she wanted to repeat, not for as long as she lived.

When homeroom started, Juliet tried to follow her mother's advice about pretending that Arturo's weird behavior of the night before had never happened. But that was hard to do when he kept staring at her.

To make the situation worse, it seemed as if some of the other boys were staring at her, too.

Stop it, she told herself. *You're imagining things!*

What she knew she was *not* imagining were the glares she was getting from Bambi Quilp and Samantha-the-Leech. But the boys were making her so nervous, she barely had time to worry about Bambi and Samantha. She wished she'd had the nerve to apologize to Bambi first thing that morning. Doing so would have been embarrassing, and painful, but at least it might have ended the situation.

At about ten o'clock, Mindy Wozinski passed Juliet a note. She assumed it was from Mindy herself, who was sort of a friend, so she was surprised to open it and find it was from Gil Jordan—officially the third cutest boy in the class, according to a secret poll taken by the girls earlier that year.

Getting a note from Gil was surprising enough. What it said was even more startling:

Juliet—
Want to sit with me at lunch?
          —Gil

Juliet glanced at Gil.

He smiled at her.

She snapped her head back to her desk, hoping her hair would cover the sudden blush that now painted her cheeks.

That was just before they went to music class. When they came back, Juliet found a piece of candy on her desk. Glancing around in puzzlement, she noticed Tyrone Jackson watching her eagerly. He smiled shyly and glanced away.

Things only got worse when the class lined up for lunch. Arturo came to stand next to her. That would have been fine, except that Gil also decided he wanted to stand next to her.

"I was here first!" said Arturo angrily.

Gil tried to push in ahead of him. Moments later they were shoving each other.

Ms. Spradling hurried over to separate them. "Looks like spring is going to be a little early this year," she said with a sigh. Then she marched the boys, who were glaring murderously at each other, out to the hall.

Juliet felt a wave of guilty relief. At least now she wouldn't have to figure out what to do about Gil's invitation to sit with him, an idea that had filled her with both delight and terror.

She sat instead, as she always did, with her best friend, Elizabeth Kennedy. Elizabeth was originally from China, and she was the only kid in the sixth grade other than Arturo whom Juliet felt really comfortable with. They had met when Elizabeth moved to Venus Harbor in second grade and had gotten to be friends because they were both so shy. Except that it had turned out that Elizabeth was only shy because she was new in town, and she got over it pretty quickly. Now she was one of the most popular kids in the class—so popular that sometimes Juliet wondered if the only reason Elizabeth stayed friends with her was out of loyalty, or worse, pity.

"What the heck is going on with Gil and Arturo?" asked Elizabeth once they were sitting down.

"I don't know," said Juliet, staring at the hunk of mystery meat on her plate. "But I don't like it."

"Are you kidding?" Elizabeth's dark eyes were sparkling. "It's like out of a story about knights and chivalry! Two guys fighting over you? What's not to like? I wish I could get a couple of guys to fight over me." She paused and looked at Juliet more carefully. "Say, did you do something to your hair? You look really pretty today."

That did it. Juliet decided that she had to say something about the amulet to Elizabeth. There was only one problem. When she opened her mouth to speak, the words wouldn't come out.

"Juliet?" asked Elizabeth. "Are you all right?"

Juliet shook her head in panic. Elizabeth leaped from her seat, ran behind Juliet, wrapped her arms around her, and gave her the Heimlich maneuver.

A burst of air shot out of Juliet's lungs.

"What are you doing?" she cried, when she had caught her breath.

"Saving you," said Elizabeth.

"From what?"

"Weren't you choking? That's what they taught us—that when someone can't get their words out, there's something caught in their throat."

Suddenly Juliet realized what was going on. *"Speak of this to no one!"* the woman in the shop had commanded.

Juliet had assumed the words to be a simple order. She had not expected that the order would be enforced by magic. With a shudder she remembered when she had started to tell her mother about the amulet that morning. Had she remained silent then out of habit... or because she was under a spell?

Juliet put a trembling hand to where the amulet lay hidden beneath her shirt.

What had she gotten herself into?

FOUR

Voices in the Attic

Things didn't get any better after lunch, mostly because Tyrone began to follow Juliet around the school yard, gazing at her longingly. He didn't get too close, and every time she stopped to glare at him, he turned away and pretended he was doing something else. Even so, she found it nerve-racking. She was embarrassed to realize that she was glad Gil and Arturo had not been allowed to come outside. She didn't think she could have coped with them acting strange, too.

"What's up with all those boys, Juliet?" asked Caitlyn Coulter, who had joined Juliet and Elizabeth at their usual spot near the bus garage. "Did you just buy the world's greatest perfume or something?"

Juliet shook her head, too confused to say anything.

The silence was filled by a familiar tapping sound. It was Terry Suss's cane. All the kids knew Mr. Suss, and there were almost as many stories about how he had lost his vision as there were kids in Venus Harbor Middle School. No matter which version you believed, it was pretty much accepted that the old man was strange but harmless. In summer he made money by sitting at a table near the beach and telling fortunes for the tourists.

The girls watched him walk toward them, white cane moving ahead of him as he checked the sidewalk for barriers. The place they were standing was about twenty feet from the sidewalk, and Juliet figured he would pass on by. But when he was directly opposite them he stopped short, then turned and began making his way across the packed dirt to where they stood. When he was a few feet away he said, "Juliet Dove?"

Prickles rose on the back of Juliet's neck. How could a blind man know where she was standing? And what did he want?

She didn't speak.

"Juliet Dove?" he asked again, his voice louder, more insistent.

"I'm here, Mr. Suss," she whispered.

He nodded. Then, in the deep voice he used for telling fortunes, he intoned:

"Past field of gold,
The key is hid.
Ignore the child,
And find the kid!

But this alone
Won't ope' the door.

The prison holds
Till mouse shall roar!

A mother's touch,
The final key,
Will break the lock
And set love free."

Juliet stared at the man in astonishment.

"What the heck is that supposed to mean?" asked Elizabeth.

But Mr. Suss had turned away. Cane tapping ahead of him, he made his way back to the sidewalk.

For a moment, none of the girls spoke. Finally Caitlyn said, "What was *that* all about?"

Juliet shook her head. "I don't have any idea," she muttered, not wanting to explain how generally weird her life had become during the last twenty-four hours—and not daring even to try explaining about the amulet.

Before Caitlyn and Elizabeth could question her further, Samantha-the-Leech came strutting up. "Hey, Killer," she sneered. "Have you apologized to Bambi for those rotten things you said yesterday?"

Juliet said nothing. She had *wanted* to apologize to Bambi. She had actually started in Bambi's direction twice that morning. She might even have been able to manage it if she could have spoken to Bambi in private. But with Samantha in full leech mode, that wasn't possible.

Having been glued to Bambi's side all day, Samantha knew very well that Juliet hadn't apologized, of course. Now she grinned evilly and said, "You've got this coming, you little witch!"

Then she raised her hand to slap Juliet's face.

Samantha moved fast, and Juliet was too astonished to duck. But Tyrone was even faster. Leaping up from behind, he grabbed Samantha's wrist, crying, "Unhand that woman!"

Samantha turned on him in fury. "Let go of me, Tyrone! Let go or I'll scream, and you'll really be in trouble."

Tyrone stared directly into her eyes. "Get away from Juliet," he said, his voice low and steady. "Get away—and stay away."

They glared at each other for a moment, neither of them moving. It was Elizabeth who broke the standoff. "You two should join the drama club," she said with a laugh. Reaching out, she took Samantha's free arm, the one not being held by Tyrone, and said, "Come here a minute, Sam. I want to talk to you."

Tyrone let go, and Elizabeth led Samantha away. Juliet watched, amazed as usual at the confident way Elizabeth could deal with people.

Suddenly she realized that Tyrone was still standing there. "Thanks," she whispered, scarcely able to look at him.

Tyrone shrugged modestly. "No problem. If Samantha gives you any more trouble, you just come get me." He paused, then asked, "You mind if I walk home with you?"

Juliet shook her head mutely, too shy to speak. Even as she did, she realized that she wasn't sure if that meant "No, don't do it!" or "No, I don't mind."

Tyrone had no such questions. "Great! See you after school!"

So they walked home together: Juliet and Tyrone...and Arturo, who had been walking home with her for years and was clearly not pleased to have Tyrone join them. To Juliet's relief, the boys talked all the way. Most of it was bragging, but it saved her from having to do any talking herself. She left them shuffling their feet awkwardly on her doorstep and hurried into the house.

"Is that you, Juliet?" called her mother. "You've got a friend here."

Juliet hurried into the kitchen. Gil Jordan was sitting at the table, a plate of Mrs. Dove's cookies in front of him. He looked miserable. "Hi, Juliet," he said.

"What are you doing here?" she asked, annoyed with herself even as she spoke for how rude she sounded. She saw her mother scowl.

"I wanted to apologize for what happened in school today," said Gil.

Juliet ducked her head. "It's all right," she murmured, wishing he would just go away.

"Well, I'd better get back to work," said Mrs. Dove cheerfully. "Got a deadline to meet!" She scurried out of the room, pausing at the door to turn and wink at her daughter.

Traitor! thought Juliet, amazed that her mother could believe she actually wanted to be alone with a boy.

As soon as Mrs. Dove was gone, Gil stood up and said, "I didn't just come to apologize, Juliet. I've been wanting to talk to you all day. I don't know what's happened, but I can't stop thinking about you. I think I'm in love with you!"

Juliet stared at him in horror. Before she could think of what to say, Gil dropped to his knees, clasped his hands in front of him, and cried, "Will you be my girlfriend?"

Juliet could feel the dreaded blush painting her face, and her heart was fluttering like a trapped bird. "Gil, stop it!" she pleaded.

"Then stop being so beautiful," he replied miserably.

That pushed Juliet over the edge. "Get on your feet, you miserable goofball. You're not in love with me, you're just making fun of me. I don't know why, but it's really, really mean of you. Stop it. Stop it now!"

To her horror, Gil burst into tears.

"Don't do that!" she cried.

"I can't help it. You're stomping on my heart!"

"That's it!" cried Juliet. "This is not a country-and-western song. Now get out of here. Go!"

"I'm sorry," moaned Gil. "I'm so, so, so, so sorry. Can't I stay? Please?"

"*Out!*" cried Juliet.

Still weeping, Gil fled. Struck by a sudden pang of guilt, Juliet turned and raced up the stairs, eager for some privacy and a chance to sort through the weird events of the day. She hurried past her own room, preferring instead to head for the attic, which was where she always retreated when she felt especially overwhelmed.

The attic had been divided into two spaces. If you turned left at the top of the stairs, you entered the

Dovecote. This was her mother's world, a studio space her parents had built for Mrs. Dove after *The Sheldons* started to become really successful.

Juliet loved the Dovecote. It was bright and airy, partly because the roof had four large windows—skylights they were called—to give Mrs. Dove lots of natural light for her work. Even better, Mrs. Dove had insisted on adding a long work space against one wall that was reserved exclusively for the children, so they could come up and do art projects while their mother was drawing. Even without talking, it was a very companionable way to spend time together.

But much as Juliet loved the Dovecote, she loved the other side of the attic even more. This was the area you entered if you turned right at the top of the stairs, and it was as raw and unfinished as the studio side was sleek and modern. Here, you could see the wooden slats of the original roof nailed to the wide timbers that supported it. Here, too, was piled the accumulated stuff—Juliet refused to call it trash, which was her father's preferred word for it—of generations.

The best stuff, of course, was from Great Aunt Bessie's world travels: boxes and bundles and trunks of things she had carried back from her journeys. When Juliet was little, Margaret used to bring her up here on "expeditions." These days Margaret didn't seem much interested in the attic, which Juliet thought was too bad.

Two years ago, shortly after the poetry jam disaster, Juliet had claimed a corner of the attic for her own. In it she had placed an old rocking chair that rocked perfectly well even though it was chipped and marred. Then she had added a shelf with some of her favorite books. And against one of the walls she had leaned a painting that Great Aunt Bessie had brought back from Greece. It showed a field of yellow flowers with a boy standing in the foreground, watching over a flock of goats. The boy had a sad look on his face that fascinated Juliet, and she had studied him over and over since she was little.

Plunking herself down in the rocker, Juliet began trying to make sense of the day's events—especially the bizarre scene with Gil just now. She placed her hand at her neck, and began tracing the chain with her fingers. It was hard to believe that the amulet could have anything to do with the crazy things that had happened. Then again, everything *had* changed since she first put it on. Should she take it off?

"Oh, don't be silly," she told herself, speaking aloud as she sometimes did in the privacy of the attic. "This amulet couldn't really make the boys act so weird." She paused, then said, "Or could it?"

"Oh, it could," said a small voice from somewhere behind her. "Believe me, it could!"

Juliet leaped to her feet. "Who said that?" she cried. She spun to look behind her. But there was no one there—at least no one that she could see.

"Don't be so frightened," said another voice. The first voice had been male; this one was clearly female. "Look, we aren't going to hurt you. We just want to talk."

"Yeah, and we had a deuce of a time finding you," said the first voice. "What the heck are you doing way up here?"

Juliet bolted across the floor, heading straight for the Dovecote. Her mother wasn't there. Heart pounding, she turned and raced down the stairs and to her own room. Slamming the door, she threw herself on the bed and stared at the ceiling, wondering if she was losing her mind.

She had just begun to catch her breath when the little male voice said, "Geez, Juliet, we told you we aren't gonna hurt you. But we do have to talk to you."

This time the voice was coming from under her bed.

FIVE

Roxanne and Jerome

Raw terror gripped Juliet's heart. For as long as she could remember, she had been afraid of what might be under her bed. Now her horrible fears about something lurking there had come true. She stared at her door, wondering if she could reach it before whatever was under the bed could grab her. She decided not to try. The bed *might* be safe territory, but once she put her feet on the floor, she knew she would be fair game.

"Are you going to come down and talk to us?" demanded the female voice. "Or do we have to come out?"

Juliet remained silent, hoping that if she didn't answer, the voices might go away.

"Did you hear me?" demanded the female. "We know you're up there, so don't try to pretend you're not! It isn't gonna do you any good!"

"How many of you are there?" asked Juliet.

"Just the two of us." This from the male. "And if you know what's good for you, you'd better talk to us."

"What are you?" asked Juliet. "Some kind of spirits?"

"Oh, *that's* a good one!" said the male. "*Us,* spirits!"

"Well, then, what are you?" Juliet persisted.

"Come on down and take a peek," said the female.

Juliet had no intention of giving whatever creatures were lurking beneath the bed a chance to drag her under there with them. Heaven alone knew where they might take her once they had her!

"You come out," she said firmly.

Instantly she regretted the words. She had read enough stories to know that magical creatures often could not enter a place until they were invited. And now she had gone and done just that.

"Wait!" she cried. "I changed my mind. Don't come out! Just talk to me from where you are!"

Her retraction was too late. She heard a rustling and a scuttering. Quaking with fear, she buried her head under the pillow to wait for the worst.

"Well, here we are!" said the male. "Sheesh, will you at least *look* at us!"

Juliet shook her head, then realized the gesture would be invisible to her unseen guests. "I can't," she said softly.

"Oh, don't be ridiculous, Juliet," said the female. "We won't hurt you. But we do have to talk to you."

"And we ain't goin' nowhere till we do," said her partner. "So you might as well get it over with."

Trembling, Juliet scooched to the edge of the bed and peered down.

"You're rats!" she cried, her voice filled with horror. Quickly she pushed herself back across the bed so she could no longer see them.

"What were you expecting?" called the male rat. "A pair of pixies? Now get back over here. My name is Jerome, this is Roxanne, and we are not—repeat *not*—going to bite you."

Juliet inched forward just far enough to peek over the edge of the bed again.

"Pleased to meetcha, Juliet," said Roxanne, standing up and waving.

Juliet slid back a couple of inches. "How do you know my name?"

"Amazing, ain't it?" said Jerome. "It's like we're psychic or somethin'."

"Impossible is more like it," said Juliet.

"Well, if it's impossible, then how come we're doing it?" asked Roxanne, crossing her little arms defiantly.

"Maybe you're not real," muttered Juliet. "Maybe I'm just losing my mind!"

"Oh, puh-leeze," said Jerome. "We don't have time to waste with monkey sauce like 'Maybe I'm crazy!' You're sane, and we're talking. Get used to it. Can we just get on with this?"

Since it was clear that whatever she said, the rats were going to keep talking, Juliet came forward just far enough to see them again.

"That's better," said Roxanne. "Now, the reason we're here is we have a message for you."

"That's our job," said Jerome proudly. "We're messenger rats."

"Who do you work for?" asked Juliet.

"The old man," said Jerome.

"What old man?"

"Mr. Elives," said Roxanne. "The man who runs the magic shop."

"You mean the place where I got the necklace?" Without realizing it, Juliet put her hand to her neck. She cried out in surprise. The amulet was warm.

"That's the place," said Jerome. "Elives' Magic Supplies, S. H. Elives, proprietor."

"Does Mrs. Elives want her pendant back?" asked Juliet. She blinked, then said in a puzzled voice, "Hey! How come I can talk to you about this?"

"What do you mean?" asked Roxanne.

"Well, I tried to tell my friend Elizabeth about the amulet today, but I couldn't say a word. It was like I was under a spell or something."

"Uh-oh," said Roxanne.

"You're not kidding," said Jerome. "But the old man warned us this thing was going to be trouble."

"So was it Mr. Elives' wife who gave me the amulet?" asked Juliet.

"Not very likely," said Roxanne, "since there is no Mrs. Elives."

"Then who was the lady I talked to?"

"We're not sure," said Jerome, his voice no longer so cocky. "That's why the old man's so nervous."

Juliet shook her head. "I don't understand. And I still don't understand why I can talk to you about this thing when I couldn't talk to Elizabeth."

"That's probably because we're magic," said Roxanne. "As for the rest of it, it's a little complicated."

"Nah, it ain't complicated," said Jerome. "It's just plain goofy. Look, here's what happened. Elives went off to do some business, and when he came back, the owl—"

"Uwila," put in Roxanne.

"Uwila," said Jerome, glaring at her, "told him what had happened when you came in the shop."

"Boy, was Mr. Elives upset!" said Roxanne. "I never saw him so mad."

"Which is going some, considering how cranky he is most of the time," added Jerome.

"I'm not sure I understand," said Juliet. "What happened?"

Jerome glanced from side to side, then said, "The short version is this: Some dame none of us ever heard of snuck into the place and gave you—well, whatever it was she gave you. And if you knew how hard it is to get into that shop, you'd understand how weird that really is."

"What's so hard about it? I just walked in."

"Have you tried going back?" asked Jerome with a smirk.

Juliet shook her head, this time a definite "no."

"Well, let's just say you're not getting back in unless the old man wants you to."

"Or unless she—whoever she is—does something again," said Roxanne, sounding distinctly nervous now.

"So does *Mr.* Elives want the necklace back?" asked Juliet, half hoping that the rats would take it from her, half wanting to never let it go.

"He can't want it *back,*" said Jerome, "on account of he never had it to begin with. There's nothing missing from the shop—and trust me, kid, he'd know if there was."

"So whatever that necklace is, it's something that woman brought in with her," said Roxanne.

"Why would someone sneak into a store just to give away something that wasn't in the store to begin with?" asked Juliet, totally confused now.

"That's what Mr. Elives wants to know!" said Roxanne. "In the meantime, he sent us to get the amulet."

"But it's mine," said Juliet, startled to hear herself claim it. "The woman gave it to me!"

Jerome sighed. "The old man doesn't want to take it away from you. He just wants to look at it, to see if he can figure out what's going on. But I gotta tell you, kid, if he says it's too dangerous to keep, I'd take his word for it."

"So if you'll just give us the amulet, we'll take it to Mr. Elives, let him look it over, and come back here to tell you about it as quick as we can," said Roxanne.

Juliet started to put her hand to her neck, then said, "Wait a minute. How do I know I can trust you? How do I know you're not trying to *steal* the amulet?"

"Geez, kid, it's not like we carry official badges or something," said Jerome. "But, if you really want to know..."

He looked questioningly at Roxanne. She nodded.

"Okay, wait a sec," said Jerome. He scurried back under the bed, only to return a moment later carrying a small envelope. Standing on his hind legs, he held it up to Juliet.

"What's this?" she asked.

"Just open it," said the rat.

Juliet reached down and took the envelope. It was not sealed. Inside was a small black-and-white photograph of an old man standing at a counter. She recognized the counter by the cash register with the owl perched on top. It was the counter at the back of the magic shop.

"Tell it your name," said Jerome.

"What?" asked Juliet, thinking she had misheard him.

"Your name," said Roxanne impatiently. "Say your name to the picture."

"What for?"

"Just do it, will ya?" said Jerome.

Juliet sighed. Holding the picture in front of her and feeling very silly, she said, "My name is Juliet Dove."

At once the image began to move. The old man looked out at her and said, "Greetings, Juliet Dove. I send you best wishes from the magic shop. I also send you apologies. I am very sorry I was not here to greet you when you came to my door."

"That's all right," said Juliet. "I wasn't—"

The voice went on speaking, and Juliet realized that he couldn't hear her. She blushed for imagining that he could have, then thought, *Well, why not? It's a magic postcard, after all!*

"I am still trying to discover who it was that *did* greet you," continued the old man. "However, I do know from Uwila here"—he gestured to the owl— "what happened while you were in the shop. It is urgent that I examine that amulet, Juliet Dove. If it is harmless, I will gladly return it to you. On the other hand, it hardly seems likely that anyone would have gone to so much trouble to get it out into the world if it were harmless.

"Now, I realize it is possible you might wonder if I am simply trying to trick you so that I can gain this powerful item for myself. But I would ask you to think back to your conversation with the woman who gave it to you. Was her manner that of someone who belonged here? Or did she seem nervous, ill at ease, in a hurry? I believe that a little reflection will assure you that something was wrong when you came into the shop.

"For your own sake, I urge you to send the amulet back to me with Roxanne and Jerome. In return, I promise to have them bring you some other, more appropriate item from my shelves—one that will almost certainly cause you less trouble than this one seems likely to."

The picture froze into immobility again, leaving the old man staring out at Juliet—though in a different position from when he had started.

Juliet sighed. "I suppose I ought to do what he asks."

"Now you're talking sense," said Jerome.

But when Juliet tried to lift the chain over her head, she found that it wouldn't fit.

"That's weird," she muttered. "I would have sworn I just slipped it over my head when I put it on."

Jerome glanced at Roxanne significantly.

Juliet reached behind her neck to unfasten the chain.

She couldn't locate the clasp.

Exasperated, she went to the mirror and pulled the chain around, planning to unfasten it from the front.

A cold chill rippled over her shoulders.

The clasp was gone.

Juliet turned the chain around and around, unable to believe her eyes. She was certain the chain had had a clasp when she put it on. Now, it seemed to have vanished. She ran the golden links through her fingers three times, hoping desperately to find a way to open it.

Nothing. The chain was an unbroken circle, with no hint it had ever been otherwise. Struggling against a wave of fear, Juliet tried one more time to slip it over her head.

Impossible.

Panic pounding through her veins, she turned to Roxanne and Jerome. "It won't come off," she whispered, her voice tight and small. *"It won't come off!"*

SIX

Clarice and Mr. Toe

Juliet stared at the mirror in horror. Was she going to have to wear this thing forever? Was the chain shrinking? What if it kept on getting smaller ... and smaller? She put her fingers to her neck, imagining the cold metal digging into her throat.

"Oh, brother," said Jerome. "The old man ain't gonna like hearing this!"

"I don't care about the old man! I want this thing off me!" She thought for a second, then said, "Wait here."

"Where are you going?" called Roxanne as Juliet headed for the door.

"To see if Margaret has some wire cutters in her art box."

"I wouldn't do that," said Roxanne.

Juliet spun around. "Why not?"

The rat spread her paws. "That chain is magic, right?"

"I dunno, Roxie," said Jerome before Juliet could

answer. "It could be just the pendant that's got the magic in it."

"Yeah, that *could* be," said Roxanne. "But it was the chain that changed size. Now I don't know a lot about magic—"

"You can say that again!"

Roxanne swatted him on the shoulder. "This is no time for smart remarks, Jerome. As I was saying, I don't know a lot about magic, but I *do* know that if you break something magic, sometimes the magic inside leaks out. Cut that chain and you might end up with magic all over the place. Given what's happened so far, I don't think that would be a good idea."

"On the other hand, odds are good that if the chain really is magic, you couldn't cut it, anyway," added Jerome.

"Then what am I going to do?" wailed Juliet.

Roxanne stood on her hind legs and studied Juliet more closely. "Has anything unusual happened since you put on the chain?"

"Nothing much," said Juliet, trying to sound casual. She waited a second, then confessed, "Some of the boys have been acting a little strange."

"Boys always act strange," said Roxanne, glancing at Jerome. "Be more specific."

Juliet felt herself begin to blush.

"This is *important*," said Roxanne.

"Well, they seem to think I'm—" she hesitated, afraid she would sound as if she were bragging.

"What?" asked Jerome. "They think you're what?"

"Pretty," said Juliet softly.

"But you *are* pretty," said Roxanne, sounding genuinely surprised. "I said that to Jerome the first time we saw you. 'That Juliet Dove is a pretty girl,' I said."

"Well, none of the boys ever seemed to think so. At least not until today. Now all of a sudden they're . . . I don't know. They keep talking to me. And following me around!"

"Uh-oh," said Roxanne.

"Extremely uh-oh," said Jerome.

Juliet looked at them in alarm. "What is it?" she asked. "What's happening?"

"Pull my whiskers if I know," said Jerome. "But I don't like the sound of it. We better tell the old man about this."

"You go," said Roxanne. "I'll stay and talk to Juliet."

Jerome paused to think this over, then said, "Okay. See you in a bit." He scampered back under Juliet's bed.

"Is there a rat hole down there?" Juliet asked nervously.

"Of course not," said Roxanne. "Your parents aren't the kind to have rats."

"Well, you're here."

"*We* are not normal rats! We are of the Immortal Vermin! Jerome just didn't want you to watch him leave. The way we go places, it's . . . well, it's sort of strange."

As far as Juliet was concerned, the whole world was suddenly a lot stranger than she had imagined. This feeling only grew more intense when she said,

"Maybe we should have all gone back to the magic shop together," and Roxanne replied, "I don't think you could get there now."

"What do you mean?"

"Well, it kind of moves around. Would you mind if I got on your desk? It would be easier to talk that way."

"I suppose it's all right. Do you want me to lift you up?"

"Nah, I'll climb."

Juliet was a little startled by how easily Roxanne scrambled up the front of her desk. Once the rat was settled, Juliet said, "What do you mean the shop 'moves around'?"

"You never saw it before, did you?"

Juliet shook her head.

"And how long have you lived in this town?"

"All my life."

"Well, there you go! It wasn't here. Then it was. Now it's probably not again. Mr. Elives keeps moving the place." Roxanne lowered her voice. "Some days I don't think we're anywhere. *That* can be a little scary, let me tell you!"

"I can imagine," said Juliet sympathetically. She paused, then, remembering what her mother had taught her about guests, said, "Uh, would you like something to eat?"

"That would be very nice," said Roxanne. She folded her paws in a prim fashion.

"Cheese, I presume?"

Roxanne sighed. "I'm not a cartoon character, you know."

"Sorry. So, what would you like?"

"Oh, I'll eat most anything. And I didn't mean to be rude. It just gets a little boring, everyone thinking all we eat is cheese, cheese, cheese."

"I'll be right back."

When Juliet returned a few minutes later, she was carrying a plate that did have some cheese on it, but also some crackers, a stalk of celery, and a Twinkie. She found Roxanne studying a picture of the Dove family that had been taken while they were on vacation the previous summer. "Nice lookin' bunch," said the rat.

Juliet smiled.

Roxanne began to eat, nibbling daintily at the things Juliet had brought. Juliet noticed that she saved the cheese for last. *Like dessert,* she thought to herself.

"That was very nice," said Roxanne, as she finished off the last of the cheese. "Thank you."

"You're welcome," said Juliet. Then, to ward off any questions about herself, she said, "How come you and Jerome can talk?"

Roxanne paused, as if deciding whether to answer. Finally, she said, "You know that old story about the woman who had two daughters, and one of them was nice to an old lady in the woods, and when the girl came home diamonds fell out of her mouth, so the woman sent the other daughter out, but she was rude to the old lady in the woods, and when she came back toads and rats and snakes fell out of her mouth?"

"Sort of," said Juliet uneasily.

"Well, me and Jerome are two of those rats. That's why we can talk; we were born out of the daughter's words."

"But that story's just made up!"

"That's strange, 'cause if that story's just made up, then I'm not here. And if I'm not here, I couldn't be talking to you. And I could have sworn that I'm standing right here talking to you!"

"But even if it is true, it happened hundreds of years ago."

"Not actually," said Roxanne, sounding a little uneasy. "Me and Jerome come from a more recent version. Sort of like a sequel. But we *could* be hundreds of years old! Us creatures that come into being that way tend to live forever. Unless we get run over by a truck or eaten by a cat or something. That's the reason we're called the Immortal Vermin: We're talking rats who live forever! Kinda cool, dontcha think?"

"I suppose so," said Juliet. "But what—"

"That's enough about us," said Roxanne quickly. "The old man doesn't like us to talk about ourselves too much. He says a little mystery is the spice of life."

"I don't like spice," said Juliet firmly.

"Not even salt?"

Juliet wavered, but finally had to admit that she did indeed like salt.

"Well, there you go. Same difference. You wouldn't wanna go through life without any salt, would you? It's the same with mystery. A few unanswered questions make life more interesting."

"All right, all right. I get your point. I was just

trying to make conversation. If you can't talk about yourself, what are we supposed to talk about?"

"We could talk about you."

Juliet shrugged. "What's to talk about? I'm just a kid."

"Personally I find kids very interesting, never having been one myself."

Juliet looked at the rat suspiciously. "What do you mean you were never a kid?"

"Well, me and Jerome came out, you know, full grown." Roxanne paused, as if remembering something. Then her face got angry. "Now there you go again, trying to get me to talk about myself! Next thing you know you'll be asking about some of the jobs me and Jerome...Jerome and I...have done."

"Sure. That would be interesting."

"Of course it would be interesting! We've had some real doozies, let me tell you. But I can't tell you. That's what I'm telling you!"

They were quiet for a moment while Juliet tried to sort out that last speech.

"Sorry," said Roxanne finally. "I didn't mean to yell at you. Maybe I should just go under the bed and wait for Jerome."

"It's all right," said Juliet. "I don't usually talk to new people that much, anyway."

"Well, it's good to be a listener. Even so, you need to throw something in yourself every once in a while to keep the conversation going, you know what I mean? Tell you what: Let's practice. You tell me one interesting thing about yourself. Just one."

Juliet blushed and shook her head.

"Oh, for Pete's sake, Juliet. It's one thing to be modest, but this is ridiculous!"

Juliet took a deep breath. "I'm in sixth grade," she said at last.

"I said tell me something *interesting*! What's your favorite book? Do you like any boys? Have you got a secret? Did you ever do something really naughty? Who in the whole world would you invite to dinner if you could? Sheesh, I'll bet there's a billion interesting things you could tell me. But 'I'm in sixth grade' *isn't* one of 'em!"

Juliet was saved from having to think of something interesting about herself by the return of Jerome, who came scooting out from under her bed. He climbed onto Juliet's desk as easily as Roxanne had. Juliet noticed that he had a roll of paper strapped to his back. But before she could ask him about it, he pointed to the empty plate and said, "Geez, Roxanne, you could have left some for me!"

"Well excu-uuse me. It's not like I knew when you were comin' back. You mighta been there for hours! Sheesh."

"I can get more," said Juliet quickly. "Just tell me what Mr. Elives said."

Jerome looked very serious. "He said a lot of things, most of which were not appropriate for the ears of a young lady. But what it came down to was this: He don't know what's going on, but whatever it is, he don't like it." The rat paused, then added, "He doesn't think you're in any danger—"

"Danger?" squeaked Juliet.

"He doesn't think there's any danger," continued

Jerome severely. "But he wants you to be careful. Also, he wants me and Roxanne to stay with you for the time being, just in case the situation gets out of hand."

Juliet gaped at him. "He wants you to *stay* with me?"

"In case the situation gets out of hand."

"Does that mean you'll be able to help me?" asked Juliet nervously.

"Nah, we probably wouldn't do you any good. But at least we'll be able to tell the old man what happened."

"Great. Why don't you get a little camera, too, so you can give him pictures. And just what does he mean by 'out of hand'?"

Jerome shrugged. "He didn't specify. But he did send you this note." He removed the roll of paper that was strapped to his back and extended it to Juliet. As she reached for it, she heard a small voice say, "Who are you talking to, sister?"

Juliet spun around. Clarice was standing in the doorway. Before Juliet could tell her little sister to go away, Clarice came trotting into the room.

"Are you all right, Juliet?" Her eyes widened. "Hey, you've got rats! Did you ask Mommy if you could have them?"

Juliet glanced over at the desk. Roxanne was standing on her hind legs, frantically shaking her head and putting one paw over her mouth. It took Juliet a second to realize that the rat was signaling for her not to say anything about them talking. "I'm, uh, taking care of them for someone."

"Can I hold one?"

Juliet turned toward the desk again. Jerome had his paws over his eyes and was shaking his head. Roxanne sighed and shrugged.

"I guess it's all right," said Juliet. "Just be gentle."

"You were talking to them, weren't you?" asked Clarice, scooping up Roxanne and stroking her back.

Juliet panicked. "Well, I—"

"Just like I talk to Mr. Toe!" said Clarice triumphantly.

Jerome scowled. Juliet wasn't sure if it was because Roxanne was getting stroked—or because he wasn't. She didn't want him to feel left out. But she also didn't think she should just pick him up. Finally, she decided to put her hand on the desk, as a sort of invitation. Jerome could decide whether he wanted to climb on or not.

He stared at her hand for a moment, then scurried up to her shoulder. But it wasn't attention he was after. Once he was close enough he put his head to her ear and whispered, "Ditch the kid."

But it was not easy to get rid of Clarice when there was something new and exciting in your room, and it was clear that she put the rats in that category.

"Let's go show them to Mommy," said Clarice after a few minutes.

"No!" said Juliet quickly. Then, more cautiously, "You know how cranky she gets if we interrupt her while she's working."

"You didn't tell Mommy you've got rats, did you?" asked Clarice, her eyes dancing.

Juliet sighed. She loved Clarice, but she also knew

that her little sister was not above blackmail. She could extract a heavy price for agreeing to keep a secret. "If Mommy finds out, I might have to get rid of them," Juliet said desperately. Then, fearing that wasn't enough, she added, "She might make me take them to the cat food factory, so they can be ground up to feed kitties."

Clarice's lower lip started to tremble and she tightened her hand over Roxanne's back. "She wouldn't!"

Juliet shrugged. "It's hard to say. People get funny ideas about rats sometimes."

"I won't tell, Juliet. I promise!"

"Thanks. Now, why don't you go play with Mr. Toe. I've got some things I have to do."

"I can't. I have to give you something."

"What is it?" asked Juliet, who was starting to lose patience.

"A letter."

Juliet furrowed her brow. "Who's it from?" she asked, wondering if one of the boys was trying to use Clarice to get to her. When Clarice didn't answer right away, Juliet felt her anger begin to rise. If one of those boys had frightened Clarice...well, she didn't know what she would do. But it wouldn't be pretty. "Who's it from?" she asked again.

"Mr. Toe."

Juliet relaxed. Clarice was always scribbling on pieces of paper and saying they were notes from Mr. Toe. She held out her hand, knowing she had to play the game before she could get back to the real problem.

Clarice pulled a carefully folded piece of paper out of her pocket. Printed on it in blue crayon, the letters large and clear, were the words "For Juliet Dove."

Juliet scowled at her little sister. "Who wrote this?"

Clarice's lip began to tremble again. "I told you! It's from Mr. Toe."

"Who *really* wrote it?" asked Juliet. She felt like she was being mean, but it was important.

"I did," confessed Clarice, a tear spilling down her cheek.

Juliet stared at her sister. She had seen Clarice's "writing" plenty of times. It was just scratchy marks.

"Clarice," she said gently, "you have to tell me who wrote this."

"I did!"

"Clarice!"

"I held the crayon! But..." Clarice looked at the floor.

"But *what*?"

Clarice sighed. "But Mr. Toe moved my hand."

SEVEN

Strange Messages

Her spine prickling with fear, Juliet stared at the note, then at Clarice, then at the note again. Finally she said, "What do you mean, Mr. Toe moved your hand?"

"He just made it move," Clarice replied. She held out her hand, as if to demonstrate.

Before Juliet could ask more, Byron came barreling into the room. "Hey, Jules, you'd better come downstairs. There's a bunch of guys outside who—" He broke off in midsentence. "You've got rats!" He paused, then asked, "Does Mom know? And where's the cage? You've got to have a cage for them."

Juliet noticed that this last statement caused Jerome to shudder.

Byron stepped toward her. "Can I hold one?"

"Can you keep them a secret?"

"Sure," he said, scooping Jerome off Juliet's shoulder. "But I'm not the one you've got to worry about. If you want to keep them secret you probably shouldn't have told Clarice."

"That's not nice," said Clarice, sticking out her lower lip.

"Wow," said Byron, ignoring her protest and focusing his attention on Jerome. "This guy's pretty chunky."

Jerome glared at him.

"Where'd you get them, anyway?" continued Byron.

"I'm taking care of them for someone," said Juliet, repeating the story she had told Clarice. "It's just for a little while."

"Aren't you worried Queen Baboo might try to eat them?"

"Who the heck is Queen Baboo?" demanded Roxanne. Then she gasped and clapped her paws over her snout.

"Aw, geez, Roxanne," said Jerome. "Can't you ever keep your trap shut? Now look what you've gone and done!"

Byron and Clarice stared from Roxanne to Jerome in amazement. An awful silence filled the room. Finally, Byron took a deep breath. Moving slowly and carefully, he put Jerome on the desk, then backed away. "Juliet," he whispered hoarsely, "did those rats just talk?"

It was Jerome who answered. Standing on his hind legs, the rat snarled, "Yeah, kid, we talked. We're both talkers. What about you? You a talker? Or do you know how to keep your mouth shut? I gotta tell ya, that's probably the smart thing to do under the circumstances!"

Byron turned to Juliet, his eyes wide with fear. He opened his mouth, but nothing came out.

"It's all right," said Juliet. "I can't tell you everything that's going on. I don't even know what's going on, completely. But they're nice rats. Really. They won't hurt you. Will you?" she added fiercely, turning to glare at Jerome.

"Not if he don't get out of line," said Jerome.

"Oh, stop, Jerome," said Roxanne. "What I want to know is, who is Queen Baboo?"

"She's a cat," said Clarice. "She belongs to our sister Margaret. She's fat. The cat, I mean. Not Margaret."

"A cat!" cried Jerome. "You didn't tell us there was a *cat* here!"

"You didn't ask!" said Juliet. "And I didn't even think about it until now. She's not my cat. And it's not like I called you up and asked you to come over!"

Byron swallowed hard, then whispered, "Juliet, do you *know* these rats?"

"Only a little. We just met."

Her brother blinked again. "Things are getting awful weird around here."

"Don't worry, kid," said Jerome. "You'll get used to us quick enough."

Byron shook his head. "It's not just you." He turned to his sister. "I came up to tell you that there's a whole crowd of boys standing in our front yard."

"What are they doing?" asked Juliet.

"They're not *doing* anything. They're just standing there, staring at the house. I think they're all from your class."

"Oh, brother," muttered Jerome. "You'd better read those notes, Juliet. Things *are* getting weird around here."

Byron shook his head. "When a talking rat thinks things are getting weird, they must *really* be getting weird!"

Juliet sighed. Jerome was right: She had to read the messages. The thing was, she was afraid to find out what they might say.

"Which one first?" she asked at last.

"I'd start with the one from Mr. Elives," said Roxanne. "At least we know who he is!"

With trembling fingers Juliet reached for the note Jerome had brought, which had rolled up again while they were talking. Across the top of the page, in large letters, were the words "IMPORTANT INFORMATION FOR JULIET DOVE." Beneath that, in somewhat smaller letters, it said: "Ignore at Your Own Peril."

"That doesn't sound good," said Juliet nervously.

"Ah, he always writes stuff like that," said Jerome.

The handwriting was thin and spidery, and a little shaky. Juliet read on.

Dear Miss Dove,

First, let me apologize again for not being able to greet you when you visited my shop. It seems the consequences of that visit, and of my absence, may be even greater than I feared.

Despite my efforts, I have not yet been able to determine who gave you that piece of jewelry, or why she did so. But that it is dangerous, possibly even treacherous, I have no doubt. That you have already begun to wear it is a matter much to be regretted.

I do not believe the chain will grow any tighter. However, the fact that you cannot remove the necklace makes it clear you have become trapped in a story. Once that happens you may not turn back without grave consequences. Your only way out now is to go forward. What, exactly, that will mean I am not certain. But you have my word that I am urgently attempting to discover what is behind all this. In the meantime I offer three pieces of advice.

First: Make a trip to the library. You may find unexpected assistance there.

Second: The key is in the key. That is, you must find the key to the amulet if you are to free yourself from its hold.

Third: Do not walk widdershins around your house between midnight and dawn.

One final note: You may trust Roxanne and Jerome. They are good and faithful rats.

I deeply regret that you have been placed in this unfortunate situation, and I hope we will be able to rectify it before long. Until we do, I advise you to be wise, wary, and watchful.

Very truly yours,
S. H. Elives

"What the heck does 'widdershins' mean?" asked Byron, when Juliet had finished reading the note out loud.

"Wrong way around," said Jerome.

"Or counterclockwise," added Roxanne.

Juliet looked at them. "How do you know that?"

The rats looked at each other and shrugged. "How do we know anything?" said Roxanne, after a moment. "It's sort of a mystery."

"So are these directions," said Juliet. "I have no idea which way around the house would be the *wrong* way, much less which way would be counter-clockwise."

"It's easy," said Byron. "If you look at the house from the top, and think of the front door as being twelve, then if you were facing the house, going to the right would be counterclockwise."

Juliet made a face. "You are in serious danger of growing up to be a top-notch world-class geek."

"It's my highest ambition."

"My advice is not to walk around the house after midnight at all," said Roxanne. "No matter which di-rection you go."

"That does seem like the best idea," said Jerome, nodding sagely.

"Read the other note," said Byron. "This is getting exciting."

"That's because you're not the one it's happening to," said Juliet.

"Well, I wish I was!"

"Oh, you *want* guys following you around and get-ting all moony over you?"

"Not *that*. But at least it's sort of an adventure. It's sure not boring!"

Juliet shook her head and picked up the note Clarice had given her.

"Read it aloud," said Clarice.

"Don't you know what it says?" asked Juliet.

"I can't read!" Clarice answered, sounding indignant.

"But you wrote it."

"Did not," said Clarice, shaking her head. "I told you, Mr. Toe wrote it. I just held the crayon."

Juliet shivered, then unfolded the paper. The note, written in the same blue crayon as her name on the outside, said:

Dear Juliet Dove,

It is urgent that I speak with you. Please meet me tonight behind your house. I will wait in the same place you saw me last night. Do not come until all are asleep. Until then, let wisdom be your guide.

—A Friend

"'A Friend'?" sputtered Juliet. "What the heck does that mean? Why didn't she just write her name?"

"Mr. Toe isn't a she!" protested Clarice.

"Well, the person I saw behind the house last night sure was," said Juliet. She shuddered. "I don't even want to think about how she got you to write this. But what's this 'A Friend' stuff? Why didn't she just write her name?"

"Maybe it's a secret," said Roxanne.

"Maybe she thought it would scare you," said Jerome.

"Maybe she's not really a friend," said Byron.

Juliet sighed. "Well, at least this should be interesting."

"You mean you're really going to go out to meet her?" asked Byron. He sounded surprised.

"I think I have to."

"Cool. Can I come, too?"

Juliet shook her head. "The note says, 'Do not come until all are asleep.' You can't come with me if you're asleep."

"Rats!" said Byron. Then, looking at Roxanne and Jerome, he added quickly, "Sorry."

"I should think so!" said Jerome stiffly. He turned to Juliet. "You don't have to do this alone. Me and Roxanne will come with you. When it says, 'Do not come until all are asleep,' I'm pretty sure it means your family members."

"Jerome's right," said Roxanne. "Trust me, we know about this kind of stuff."

"Thanks," said Juliet. "It'll be good to have you with me." She took a deep breath. "Okay, I'm heading for the library."

"Not without us you're not," said Jerome. "The old man wants us to watch out for you, and that's what we're gonna do!"

"I can't take a pair of rats into the library with me," said Juliet.

"Isn't that just like humans," muttered Roxanne in disgust.

"I'm sure that if all rats were like you and Jerome that rule would be different," said Juliet.

"No doubt," replied Roxanne. "Even so, I would

prefer to be judged as an individual, *not* as a member of a group!"

"How about if I take you in my backpack?" suggested Juliet, who truly did not want to get into a political discussion with a pair of talking rats.

"Can you make it comfy?" asked Jerome.

"And maybe put in a few snacks?" added Roxanne.

Juliet smiled. "I think we can manage that."

Byron and Clarice insisted on coming along, too, of course. Once the rats were settled and the children were ready, they went to the front door. But when Juliet opened it, she cried out in dismay.

Every boy in her homeroom was gathered there, staring dreamily at the doorway.

A great cheer went up when they saw her.

Juliet ducked back into the house and slammed the door behind her.

EIGHT

Tales of the Gods

"What am I going to do?" wailed Juliet. "I can't go out there with all those boys!"

"I told you they were there," said Byron.

"What is it?" demanded Jerome. "What's going on?"

Byron leaned over and put his face close to the backpack. "Mob of boys waiting for Juliet," he whispered. "We've got to take another route." Straightening up, he said, "Let's use the back door."

Margaret was in the kitchen, scraping up old linoleum, when the three younger Doves came in. "Hey, why don't you grab a tool and give me a hand?" she asked sweetly.

"Because Dad's paying you and he didn't offer to pay us," answered Byron immediately. "Besides, we've got something else to do right now." Moving aside some tools that Margaret had stacked in front of the door, he opened it, peered out, then whispered, "The coast is clear!"

Quickly Juliet and Clarice followed him out the door.

"Now what?" said Juliet. "We still can't go out front. Even if we could, I don't want to take a chance on going the wrong way."

"Huh?" asked Byron.

"You know," said Juliet. "Widdershins."

Byron sighed. "I told you how to figure out which way that is. But it doesn't matter. We don't have to go out front. We can go through Arturo's yard." Seeing the look on his sister's face, he added, "Don't worry— Arturo's probably in front of our house with the rest of the Venus Harbor love squad."

"I don't know," said Juliet uneasily. "I don't re-member seeing him there."

And, indeed, when they went through the hedge into the Perezes' backyard, they found Arturo sitting in a lawn chair, staring longingly at their house. He leaped to his feet. "Juliet! Thank goodness you're here! I'm sorry about last night. I'm sorry about this afternoon. I'm sorry about—"

"It's all right!" she said urgently. "Just be quiet for heaven's sake!"

"What are you up to?" asked Arturo, lowering his voice.

"We're going to the library!" said Clarice happily. "Mr. Toe is coming, too!"

Arturo gravely bent to shake hands with Mr. Toe, as he always did when Clarice said he was around. Juliet had tried to shake hands with Mr. Toe once, but Clarice had said sharply, "He doesn't have hands for you. Only for Arturo!"

Mr. Toe properly acknowledged, Arturo asked, "Do you mind if I come along?"

Juliet could find no good reason to say no. So Arturo joined them, managing to station himself next to Juliet as they walked. He kept looking at her sideways, until she wanted to smack him one and tell him to stop.

It's not his fault, she kept telling herself. *It's not his fault. It's this darn amulet!*

They had gone three blocks before the other boys figured out where they were and came running up. None of them spoke; they just followed along a few feet behind her. But every time Juliet glanced over her shoulder, she saw that they were staring at her with longing.

"It's like a parade," muttered Byron.

Juliet wouldn't have minded, except that about two blocks from the library, they passed Bambi Quilp and Samantha-the-Leech. The girls were on the other side of the street and did not bother Juliet. But she could tell from the expression on their faces that the trail of boys behind her had not gone unnoticed. She was pretty sure that she would suffer for it later.

The librarian at the main desk looked startled—and a little worried—when they all walked in together. Pretending that she didn't know the boys were following her, Juliet headed straight for the kids' section of the library.

The boys trailed silently behind.

Juliet was surprised to find that Ms. Priest, the woman who had come to dinner the night before, was on duty. Leaving the boys to fend for themselves, Juliet walked quickly up to the desk.

"Good afternoon, Juliet," said Ms. Priest. "How nice to see you again."

Juliet forced down a sudden wave of shyness. "Nice to see you, too," she replied. As she spoke, she remembered Ms. Priest's strange statement of the night before: "I expect we will get to know each other very well in the days to come." She looked at the librarian more closely. Was it possible she knew something about what was going on?

"Can I help you with anything?" prompted Ms. Priest.

"I hope so. I got a message that told me I should come here."

"That's interesting. Who was the message from?"

"A man named Mr. Elives."

"Ah. Then it is probably very good that you followed his advice. What did he want you to speak to me about?"

Juliet paused, then fished the amulet from under her shirt and whispered, "I'm having some trouble with this piece of jewelry."

She was slightly startled that she was able to speak of the amulet at all, but figured it must be because, like Roxanne and Jerome, Ms. Priest had some connection to the magic shop.

The librarian glanced at the pack of boys clustered about ten feet away. "I see," she murmured. "Goodness, this is a bit of a problem."

"I'm supposed to unlock it, I think," said Juliet. "Only I don't have the key."

"May I study it more closely?"

Juliet looked from side to side, then whispered, "I can't take it off!"

Ms. Priest's eyes widened. Then, with a nod, she bent her head to examine the amulet. When she looked up again, her face was very serious. "Though we librarians are, in many ways, the keepers of the keys, I know nothing of the key for this strange item. I must do some research, Juliet. It will require books from my own collection—ones we don't have here in the public library. If I find anything significant, I'll come by your house with it this evening, if that's all right with you."

Juliet nodded. Then, on impulse, she said, "This Mr. Elives...is he a good man?"

The librarian paused, then smiled. "Yes. Yes, I would say that he is. Somewhat strange, and fairly crotchety. But, overall, a good man. I work with him sometimes. Not always—I have my own path to follow. But on occasion we join forces."

"Doing what?" asked Juliet eagerly.

"Let's just say that I act as a guide." Then, clearly ending the conversation, she said, "If I find anything, I will see you later this evening. In the meantime I would advise you to be wise, wary, and watchful."

"Thank you," said Juliet, a little startled by the abrupt way the conversation ended. "I'll see you then, I hope."

As she turned to go, a tiny voice behind her said, "Hey, Hyacinth! How ya doin'?"

"Jerome!" said another voice. "Be *quiet*!"

Juliet spun back around. Ms. Priest looked at her

with a raised eyebrow. "That's a very interesting back-pack," was all she said.

"You're not kidding," said Juliet.

The boys followed her home, of course, and twice there were near fights, which Juliet prevented only by speaking sternly to Gil and Arturo. She was surprised she was able to do that, but the thought of them actually fighting over her was even more horrifying than the thought of saying something about it. She left them clustered at her doorstep, gazing at her lovingly. Once inside she hurried up to her room, Clarice and Byron close at her heels.

"Boy, whatever that amulet is, it really does work," said Byron once they had closed the door. "It's like you're a total love magnet or something!"

"Just shut up about it, will you?" snapped Juliet, fumbling with the straps on her backpack. She put the pack on her bed and Roxanne and Jerome scrambled out, looking somewhat worse for the wear. Jerome shook his head and began scratching behind his right ear.

Before Juliet could decide what to do next, a voice from the attic called, "Juliet? Come on up, would you, sweetheart? I need you to model for me."

"It's my mother," explained Juliet to Roxanne and Jerome. "I have to go." She left the room, frustrated at being called away and at the same time relieved at the chance for a break from the weirdness.

Juliet always had mixed feelings about posing for her mother. She liked helping out. But the character her mother had her posing for was actually based on Juliet herself. It was not easy for a shy person to have a comic strip version of herself sent all over the country.

It didn't help things any when her mother said, "Juliet, are you sure you can't bring yourself to enter the poetry jam? It would mean the world to your father."

"Don't you remember what happened that first year? It was only the most embarrassing moment of my entire life!"

"You know what they say about falling off a horse," said Mrs. Dove, without looking up from her drawing board. "The best thing to do is to get back on and ride again."

"That's if you want to ride at all," said Juliet bitterly.

Mrs. Dove sighed. "Juliet, I want you to be a strong and powerful woman when you grow up. If you can't speak in public, it's almost like being mute." She reached for an eraser. "Hold still for just a minute. I need you to keep that pose!"

She drew for a few minutes longer. Then, speaking casually, she said, "Is something going on with you and the boys, Juliet? There's an awful lot of messages for you on the answering machine."

Juliet tried to speak, but no words would come, so she just shook her head. Mrs. Dove, used to getting this response to her questions, had no idea it was because her daughter was under a spell.

By the time Juliet was finished posing, it was time for supper. Because of the kitchen floor project,

Mr. Dove had brought home food from the Chinese takeout restaurant—a great relief to the younger Doves, who always approached dinner with a certain amount of nervousness.

Before Juliet could return to her room, there was yet another interruption: Ms. Priest arrived, carrying a small leatherbound book.

"I brought this for Juliet," she said when Mrs. Dove had invited her in for coffee. "I thought she might be interested in some of the stories it contains."

"*Tales of the Gods,*" read Mr. Dove, glancing at the cover of the book.

Ms. Priest nodded. "Juliet needed some specialized information about the Trojan War."

Mr. Dove's face lit up. "Ah, great stuff! Helen of Troy! The face that launched a thousand ships."

"What is *that* supposed to mean?" asked Margaret.

"It's from a play by Christopher Marlowe, who might have grown to be as good as Shakespeare if he hadn't gotten himself stabbed in a tavern brawl," said Mr. Dove. "It's about this guy named Dr. Faustus who makes a deal with the devil. In return for his soul, he asks for the most beautiful woman who ever lived, who happens to be Helen of Troy." Mr. Dove had his poetry-quoting look in his eyes. "'Was this the face that launch'd a thousand ships, and burnt the topless towers of Ilium?'"

"How can towers be topless?" asked Margaret. "Did they forget to finish them?"

"It's poetic license," said Mr. Dove, looking as if he

had bitten down on something very sour. "Marlowe is simply saying that the towers were very tall."

"Easier ways to get the point across," said Margaret, pouring herself a cup of coffee.

"Easier, but not as beautiful," said Ms. Priest softly.

"But what's it all about?" asked Byron. "Who was Helen of Troy, anyway?"

"The most beautiful woman who ever lived," repeated Mr. Dove. "Except for your mother, of course."

"Wisely spoken," said Ms. Priest.

Mr. Dove turned to his children. "Have you really never heard of Helen?"

The younger Doves shook their heads.

Mr. Dove sighed. "Things are not as they used to be. I don't know who to blame for this dreadful lapse in your education—myself, or the school. I think I'll run for the school board next year. Do you suppose I could get elected on the motto 'Less self-esteem, more poetry!'?"

"Unlikely, dear," said Mrs. Dove, patting his arm.

Margaret scowled at him. "If you even *think* about doing that before I graduate, I swear I'll never speak to you again."

"Not even to ask for money?" asked Mr. Dove hopefully.

Ms. Priest turned to the children. "I don't really have the story prepared. But I could tell you the broad strokes of it if you'd like."

"Please!" said Juliet, who suddenly felt it was very important.

"Very well. Helen of Troy was the most beautiful

woman in the world. But the story starts before that. Actually the story starts, as all stories do in their way, with the very beginnings of the world, for in that time were spun the threads that stretch forward to this very moment. Take anything in the now, and if you have the eyes to follow it, it can lead you all the way back to the beginning.

"But that's a bit too far for our purposes, so let's just say that the beginning in this case was the wedding of Thetis and Peleus, which was a great event to which most of the gods were invited. Most, but not all—for one goddess, Eris by name, was not invited."

"Why did they leave her out?" asked Clarice.

Ms. Priest tilted her head. "Eris was the goddess of discord, and so brought strife wherever she went. And who wants discord at a wedding? But discord came, anyway. Angered at being left out, Eris made her presence known by tossing a golden apple labeled 'For the Fairest' into the midst of the party."

"That sounds like she was being nice," said Byron.

"Not really. There was only one apple, and many goddesses, and naturally each of them wanted to be seen as the most beautiful of all. In the end, it came down to three main claimants: Hera, queen of the gods; Athena, goddess of wisdom; and Aphrodite, goddess of love."

"I thought Venus was the goddess of love!" said Clarice, who was very proud of living in Venus Harbor.

"The gods and goddesses have gone by many names," said Ms. Priest. "The Greeks called the goddess of love Aphrodite; the Romans named her Venus. Yet both groups told many of the same stories about her. Anyway, after a period of quarreling, the three goddesses asked Zeus—he was the king of the gods—to choose who should receive the apple. But Zeus was far too smart for that; he knew that in choosing he would please one goddess but anger the other two so deeply that they would make his life an ongoing misery. Finally he convinced them to ask a mortal to judge. They decided on a lad named Paris, a prince of Troy who was at that time living as a shepherd. Unfortunately, the goddesses were not content to let the lad choose on his own. So each of them tried to bribe him."

"They're not very well behaved for goddesses," observed Margaret.

"All too human, in their way," agreed Ms. Priest. "Now, Hera would have given the young man great wealth, and Athena promised victory in any battle— for that as well as wisdom was in her power. But those things paled next to the offer of Aphrodite, who said that if Paris picked her, she would provide him with the most beautiful woman on Earth to be his wife. Not surprisingly for a young man, Paris declared Aphrodite the winner. And the goddess, true to her bargain, arranged for Paris to wed Helen, the most beautiful woman on Earth." Ms. Priest paused, raised an eyebrow, then said, "Both of them ignored, for the time being, the fact that Helen was already married to the king of Sparta."

"Uh-oh," said Byron.

"Indeed," said Ms. Priest. "After Paris had stolen Helen from her home, Helen's husband raised a fleet of a thousand ships to attack Troy, the walled city where Paris had taken his new wife. The war between the Greeks and the Trojans raged for ten years—and ended with the total destruction of what had been the greatest city in the world."

"All for love," said Mr. Dove sadly.

"Or what passed for love," said Ms. Priest, her voice a bit more tart than usual.

"Then all for eros," said Mr. Dove.

"Eros? I thought it was *Eris* who caused all the trouble," said Juliet. She was slightly confused because her father was usually very precise about words.

Ms. Priest smiled. "Eris was the goddess of discord. *Eros* is the word the Greeks used for romantic love—and also for the god who handled that particular matter, who happened to be Aphrodite's son. Given the amount of discord caused by romantic love, I've always thought it somewhat amusing that the name Eris and the word *eros* are so similar."

"They say that the more important something is to a culture, the more words the people have for it," said Mr. Dove. "I've always wondered what it says about us that we have only one word for love."

"How many did the Greeks have?" asked Juliet.

"Well, there was *eros,* for romantic love," said Ms. Priest. "And *philia,* which was brotherly love."

Juliet and Byron looked at each other and both made a face.

"That's where Philadelphia gets its name," said

Margaret, sounding superior. "It's the city of brotherly love."

Mr. Dove beamed at his oldest daughter.

"But the highest form of love was called *agapé*," said Ms. Priest, "the selfless love of one person for another. This is not the love that desires to possess, but the love that comes from an open heart and desires the greatest good for others." She looked a little sad when she added, "Maybe the reason we don't have a separate word for such love is that it is so rare in our modern world. Or perhaps it's the other way around. Maybe the reason we're always so confused about love is that we don't have the proper words to discuss it in all its forms."

She sighed and stood. "Well, we can't cure that now. I just came to bring you this book, Juliet. It has considerably more detail about the Trojan War—and some other things you might find of interest." She seemed to put a great deal of emphasis on these last words, and she looked Juliet directly in the eye as she pressed the little volume into her hands. "It's worth reading," she said, her voice soft but insistent. Then she turned quickly away and said her good nights to the rest of the family.

"Boy, how do you rate?" asked Margaret, after Ms. Priest was gone. "Personal book delivery! I wish I could get that kind of service when I'm doing a research paper."

"If you'd start your papers on time, you wouldn't need that kind of service," said Mr. Dove, who lived in a permanent state of semi-annoyance at the fact that his oldest daughter was the kind of student who would drive him mad if she were in one of the classes he taught. "Come on, help me do some more work on that floor."

Juliet excused herself and headed for her room, hoping desperately that Ms. Priest's book might hold the secret for freeing her from the amulet.

NINE

The Other Realm

"Well, it's about time you got back here," said Jerome, when she walked in. "We were starting to worry about you."

Both the rats were sitting on Juliet's pillow—which made her glad that she had actually made the bed that morning, since it meant the pillow was covered by the bedspread.

Roxanne gave Jerome a nudge. "For heaven's sake, don't be such a nag, Jerome. She was just downstairs with her family. Weren't you, Juliet?"

"Yeah, and she brought some of 'em back with her," said Jerome, pointing to the door.

Turning, Juliet saw that Byron and Clarice had followed her upstairs.

"We want to know what's in the book, too," said Byron.

Juliet sighed, then smiled. "All right, come on in."

Soon Byron and Clarice were sitting side by side on her bed. With Roxanne and Jerome still crouched together on the pillow, Juliet felt almost as if she were on stage—not a feeling she particularly enjoyed. Positioning her desk chair so that she was facing them, she sat down and looked at the book. Three or four slips of paper protruded from its upper edge. She assumed they were simply bookmarks, until she opened to the first one and saw that it was actually a note from Ms. Priest.

The other thing she saw at the same moment—a thing considerably more startling—was that the book itself was written by hand. The writing was neat and precise, so it was easy enough to read. At first she wondered if it was someone's journal. But when she turned to the front, it had a regular title page—though no copyright page.

The title page read:

TALES OF THE GODS
A History Beyond the Myths
by S. H. Elives

Someone must have copied it over for him, she thought. *His handwriting isn't nearly this good.*

After slipping another piece of paper into the spot that had been marked by Ms. Priest, Juliet read the note.

Dear Juliet,

I was interested—and disturbed—by your visit to the library this afternoon. I spent much of the rest of the day trying to find the information you need. After consultation with Mr. Elives, and scouring my own shelves, I have come to the conclusion that the amulet you are wearing originally belonged to Helen of Troy.

If I am correct, this is an enormously powerful object, capable of causing considerable chaos—as I suspect you have already begun to realize. Mr. Elives and I are both seeking more information. In the meantime it seems that powers we once thought to be gone, or at least at rest, have caught you in their web. I have marked some sections of this book. I suggest you read them carefully.

Very truly yours,
Hyacinth Priest

"What does it say?" demanded Byron.

Juliet read the note aloud. Roxanne and Jerome glanced at each other. "This is getting weirder by the hour," muttered Jerome.

Juliet began to check through the book. The first section Ms. Priest had marked told more about the Trojan War. She read it out loud, so that they could all hear it, but though the story was interesting, she didn't think there was anything in it that applied to the current situation.

The second section was another matter. The page was labeled "Where Have the Old Gods Gone?" and Ms. Priest had marked a certain paragraph for special attention.

Now, the time came when the world turned from the old powers, who had gone by many names in many places. Thus ignored, these old ones began to retire to their own world, and in time those who had been called gods fell into a kind of sleep—a dream from which they only roused upon occasion. All, that is, save she who had been known as Eris, for she remained fascinated by humans and the trouble that she could bring to their midst—trouble from which she drew strength, and power.

Juliet continued to read aloud from the book until they heard Mrs. Dove coming to get Clarice for bed, at which point Roxanne and Jerome scrambled into a desk drawer that Juliet had left open for them to hide in. Clarice resisted going to bed, but she was asleep on her mother's shoulder before she left the room. Once they were gone, Juliet returned to reading aloud from the book. She had been reading aloud to Byron at night since he was two years old, so this was not something that aroused any attention from the rest of the family.

By the time Mrs. Dove called Byron for bed, all four of them, kids and rats alike, knew a great deal more about the Trojan War. And they had all been startled by the behavior of the gods and goddesses involved.

"Margaret was right," said Byron at one point. "They don't act very grown up for gods!"

"I guess if you're a goddess you don't have to act grown up," said Roxanne.

"That's a scary thought," said Juliet, putting her hand to where the amulet lay hidden beneath her shirt. She sighed. "I hope that woman who wants to talk to me tonight will be able to help me with this."

"I almost forgot about that!" cried Byron. "Are you still planning to go out there?"

"I have to. What if she knows how to get me out of this mess?"

"Can I come with you?" pleaded Byron.

Juliet shook her head. "'Do not come until all are asleep,'" she said, quoting the letter again.

Byron heaved a sigh. "I don't think I'll be able to *go* to sleep until I know what happens."

"You'd better, or nothing will happen at all," said Jerome.

With another sigh Byron left the room.

The night drew on. Good nights were said. The house seemed to settle in on itself. But still, Juliet could hear her parents downstairs, listening to the late news on the television. She began to fear she would fall asleep and miss her appointment with the mysterious woman.

"Don't worry," said Jerome. "Me and Roxanne will wake you up if you conk out."

As it happened, Juliet was far too excited to sleep.

Not long after midnight, the house finally did fall silent—the kind of silence that comes not only because talk and activity have ceased, but because all are asleep. Or, in this case, all but one girl and two rats.

"Okay," whispered Jerome, "let's go!"

Juliet climbed out of bed. Though she was still fully dressed, she put on a hooded sweatshirt, knowing that the night would be cool and damp. Roxanne and Jerome scrambled onto her shoulders, and they slipped quietly out of her room.

"I have to say, I'm impressed," said Roxanne as they started down the stairs. "I wasn't sure you would do this."

"Just because I'm shy doesn't mean I'm a coward," whispered Juliet.

She headed for the kitchen, planning to go out the back way. But her father and Margaret had left a pile of tools in front of the door to the outside, and Juliet didn't think she could move them without waking the rest of the house.

"Guess it's the front door after all," said Roxanne.

"What about the part about not going around the house the wrong way?" asked Juliet nervously. "I know Byron told us which way is widdershins, but I don't want to take a chance."

"Ah, that's easy," said Jerome. "We won't *go* around the house!"

"Well how am I supposed to meet this woman if we don't go around the house?"

The rat sighed. "Look, we're going to go *halfway* around the house to meet her, right?"

"I suppose so," said Juliet hesitantly.

"Stay with me on this. We go halfway around to meet her. Then when you're done talking to her, we turn and go back the way we came. That way we don't go *around* the house. As long as we don't go past the halfway mark, we're safe whichever way we go!"

"Are you sure about that?" asked Juliet suspiciously.

"Jerome is very good with this kind of thing," said Roxanne.

"If you say so," said Juliet.

She stopped at the tool drawer, grabbed a flashlight, slipped it into the pouch in the front of her sweatshirt, then tiptoed back the way she had come. Easing open the front door, she peeked out, hoping that none of the neighbors would be returning from a night on the town—and that all her moony-eyed admirers had been locked safely in their homes.

To her relief, the street was empty.

She stepped outside. The night was cool and damp, the smell of the sea strong on the air. The nearly full moon made it easy to see, despite the low mist that covered the ground.

"I still wish I could remember which way Byron said to go," she muttered uneasily.

"I told you, it doesn't make any difference, as long as we don't go more than halfway around the house," said Jerome impatiently. "The big question is, where is this dame going to meet you? If she's not directly behind the house, we should go whichever way would be shorter."

"So we don't go more than halfway," added Roxanne.

"Got it," said Juliet. She stepped off the flagstone path, turned left, and started for the backyard.

The grass was wet with dew, and soon her sneakers were as well.

When she passed the second corner of the house, the moon appeared brighter than ever, its silver light making the mist seem to glow from within.

The tulips were open again.

And there, just where she had stood before, was the mysterious woman. The woman beckoned, but for a moment Juliet stood, unmoving, uncertain. Then she relaxed. It was indeed Alvina Clark, just as her mother had suggested. But what did she have to do with all this?

Juliet started forward again. As she walked, a sudden shimmer of light surrounded Alvina. The old face seemed to flicker. Juliet wanted to run away. But somehow it was too late to turn back, and she felt herself drawn on by a power she could not resist.

As Juliet drew closer to Alvina, she felt as if she were looking at two women squeezed into one place. There was Alvina, stooped and gray, her face lined with old sorrow. Flickering over her, sometimes so brightly that Alvina disappeared altogether, was another woman, tall and proud, with a broad, high brow and clear gray eyes. In one hand she held a spear. A sudden whir of wings caused Juliet to look up. An owl dropped out of the mist to settle on the woman's shoulder. Juliet thought the talons must have hurt as the owl took its place, but the woman did not show any sign that she felt them.

"Let's stop right here," whispered Jerome. "Owls and rats are not a good combination."

"You are safe," said the woman, though she should not have been able to hear his whisper from where she stood. Her voice, rich and beautiful, seemed to come from a long way away. "My owl will not hurt you, Jerome."

"Oh, geez," muttered the rat. "I hate it when they know your name before you even talk to them."

"Who are you?" asked Juliet, barely able to speak above a whisper herself.

The woman gave her a sad smile. "I have had many names. Now I hardly know *what* to call myself. I am but a shadow of what I once was. The world continues to change, and what I represent is not much valued in these times."

"What do you represent?" asked Juliet.

"Wisdom," said the woman, who now seemed to have replaced Alvina altogether. She smiled wryly and added, "Though I have not always been wise myself."

Lifting a hand, she pointed an ivory-colored finger at the amulet that hung around Juliet's neck. "I came to warn you about that. I see I am somewhat late. It would have been better had you never put it on."

"I've already figured that out," said Juliet bitterly.

"You wear a talisman of love," said the woman. "But love must be tempered with wisdom, else it can become a force that leads to destruction."

The owl shook its wings.

"I spoke of wisdom," said the woman. "Alas, I am but a poor representative of it. I urge you to be more thoughtful than I was in the days of the golden apple. In that contest, and in the terrible years that followed, I too often let anger or envy into my heart. Those things are the enemies of wisdom, and it withers in their presence. When I most let anger rule me, I was most false to my cause. It is *agapé* that should guide you, for in its warm light, wisdom grows and thrives. Act with this in mind, Juliet Dove, and you can never go wrong."

Juliet stared at the woman in wonder. "Who are you, really?" she whispered.

The woman closed her eyes. "A shadow. A ghost. A visitor from another world, using this poor woman as a vessel to reach you, as I recently used your little sister." She smiled. "Though I have had many names, that was the first time I have been known as Mr. Toe!"

"I still don't understand," said Juliet. She felt Roxanne and Jerome shift on her shoulders.

"All right, I'll be more direct. I am she who was once called Athena." Now she looked forlorn indeed. "I was stronger in those times, if not as wise as I should have been. But then, none of us were as wise as we should have been."

"Us?" asked Juliet.

"We who were called gods. We've drawn back from the world of men these days. You don't need us anymore. But some of us have a hard time letting go. Eris—"

"Discord!" said Juliet.

Athena nodded. "Eris is always with you. She finds humans oddly attractive, partly because she loves getting them to quarrel. Not that she needs to do much in that regard; you mortals seem quite capable of creating discord on your own. That was part of why we gods withdrew from the human world. Love, war, wisdom, discord—you were generating those things at a phenomenal rate all on your own. You hardly needed our encouragement."

"I don't know," said Juliet. "I think we're still a little short on the wisdom part."

Athena smiled sadly. "Often it is not wisdom that is lacking, but will. Most people know, most of the time, what would be wisest to do. The problem is they choose to act otherwise. Or they lack courage."

Juliet blushed, thinking of the apology she had been afraid to offer Bambi.

Athena sighed. Juliet could see Alvina's face, flickering underneath that of the goddess. "There's not much I have to offer these days that humans don't already know. If I could give them the wisdom to use the wisdom they have, that would be something else altogether!"

"What about Eris? What does she have to do with me?"

"It was Eris who gave you the amulet, which had been hidden safely away for many centuries. She wants it loose in the world again because it is an incredible source of discord. You must be careful, Juliet. You have been swept up in an old story and powerful forces are moving around you. Be wise, wary, and watchful."

Juliet recognized the words, which had appeared in Mr. Elives' letter and then been repeated by Hyacinth Priest.

Athena raised her arm and the owl fluttered away, disappearing into the darkness. She was flickering again and seemed more distant. "I must go now. We have bound ourselves away from the world of men, and it is not easy for us to come back, not easy for any of us save Eris, who never really left you."

She began to fade.

"Wait!" called Juliet, not sure what else she wanted of the goddess but reluctant to have her leave. "Wait..."

Alvina Clark's face was showing through more strongly now. But Athena's eyes were still there as the flickering form leaned forward and kissed Juliet on the forehead. "Be wise," she whispered again. "Let go of fear, and act out of love."

She shimmered and vanished, leaving Alvina Clark standing in her place. The old woman looked bewildered. But she also looked radiant, as if she had just experienced something beautiful, something that filled her with joyful expectation.

"Are you all right?" whispered Juliet.

Alvina blinked. "What? Who said that?" Then her eyes seemed to focus on Juliet. "Oh, I know you! You're the Dove girl. Yes, sweetheart, I'm all right. In fact, I've never felt better in my life. But . . . oh, I don't know. I'm almost on fire. Yet I feel as if something is missing, too." She started to cry. "It's very strange, isn't it?"

"Very," agreed Juliet.

"Well, I need to go home now," said Alvina, wiping at her tears. "You should be home, too! It's late."

"Yes," said Juliet. "It's late."

She watched Alvina turn and walk into the mist that still swirled about them.

"Geez!" said Jerome. "Roxanne and me have been in some weird situations before, but this is something else."

"You're not kiddin'," said Roxanne. "Come on, Juliet. Let's get out of here."

Juliet, dazed by her second meeting with a goddess, turned to go. She hadn't walked more than five steps when Jerome cried, "Wrong way! Quick, turn back! Turn back!"

His warning came too late.

The mist grew thicker. A terrible coldness surrounded them. And then, clearly, they were somewhere else.

Somewhere they had never intended to be.

TEN

She Who Wanders

"Oh, geez," said Jerome, as the mist wrapped around them. "We're in for it now. Where do you suppose we are, anyway?"

"I don't have the slightest idea," whispered Juliet, her voice trembling. She was terrified, but also furious at herself for having made this mistake.

"Well, it sure ain't Kansas," muttered Roxanne. Juliet glanced at the rat, who was clinging to her left shoulder. Roxanne shrugged. "*The Wizard of Oz* is one of my favorite movies."

Juliet pivoted and began to retrace her steps.

"I suspect it's too late to turn back now," said Jerome.

The rat was right, as Juliet had to admit when she had walked back five paces, then ten, then twenty, then fifty, only to find the mist thicker than ever.

"Now what do we do?" she whispered, her voice husky with fear.

"I think we'd better go back in the direction you were walking before," said Jerome.

"Jerome's right," said Roxanne. "Once you start one of these things, you pretty much have to go through to the other side if you want to get out again."

"Have you ever been in 'one of these things'?" asked Juliet.

"Not really," said Roxanne. "But hanging around in the magic shop—well, you hear a lot of stories."

"I hear something *now*," said Jerome. "Listen!"

Juliet paused. In the distance she could hear waves crashing on rocks. The sound was familiar; Venus Harbor was a seashore town, after all. But it was not a sound she had ever heard from her own backyard.

"The mist seems thinner that way," said Jerome. "Maybe we better go there."

"At least I'll have a better chance of walking without tripping," muttered Juliet, who, unable to see the ground beneath the mist, had already stubbed her toe a couple of times. As she walked, the sky grew lighter. Soon they left the mist—and the darkness—behind, emerging into a sunny day. The landscape was rocky, with low-growing trees and shrubs. There was not a house or building in sight.

She started toward the waves and soon found a rocky path. It led upward, bringing them out at the edge of a cliff that was higher than anything Juliet had ever seen around Venus Harbor.

The air ahead was clear, and she stood for a moment to watch the sea roll toward shore in great combers, its surface unmarred by any ship, or buoy, or other sign of man. Far out, she saw a dolphin leap. She looked down. It was at least a hundred feet to the great rocks against which the sea was breaking in cascades of foam.

Running along the edge of the cliff was a path, not well traveled but easy enough to spot. To the right it sloped downward. To their left it made a steep climb up.

"Which way do you think we should go?" asked Juliet.

"My guess is up," said Roxanne.

"Figures," said Jerome.

"Hey, you're not the one who has to climb it," said Juliet.

"So I was being sympathetic. But if we're gonna do it, let's get going. This is making me nervous."

Juliet comforted herself with the thought that at least there were no people here. Heck, if she was lucky, maybe she could get through this without having to talk to anyone. Well, anyone except Roxanne and Jerome. She realized that right now she would be totally terrified if she were on her own. How was it that a pair of talking rats could make all this seem bearable?

They had been walking along the cliff for about ten minutes when they spotted the palace. Made of rose-colored marble, its high pillars thrust from the mist ahead of them like rays of sunlight shooting up from the earth.

"Wowza," said Jerome. "Wonder what the rent is on that baby."

"Not much," creaked a voice beside them. "Just your life."

Juliet spun toward the voice. A wizened old woman had hobbled to the edge of the path. Her hair was wispy, her skin bumpy and wrinkled, her teeth mostly gone. She extended a hand that was bent like a claw. "What nice rats," she wheezed. "Do you think I could have them?"

Jerome and Roxanne cowered back.

"Who are you?" asked Juliet. At least that was what she meant to ask. What actually came out of her mouth was little more than a squeak.

She tried again. "Who are you?"

The old woman shrugged. "People call me any number of names." She reached toward the amulet. Juliet started to pull back but Roxanne, her mouth right next to Juliet's ear, whispered fiercely, "Hold still! It's always better to be nice to an old lady in a situation like this."

Resisting the urge to point out the way Roxanne and Jerome had recoiled when the old woman first appeared, Juliet forced herself to remain still. The woman lifted the amulet in her twisted fingers and bent her head to examine it.

"Very pretty," she crooned at last. "And oh-so-dangerous. I think you had better go on into the palace."

And with that she vanished.

Juliet blinked.

"People come and go in the strangest way here," said Roxanne, referring to *The Wizard of Oz* again.

"Should we do what she said?" asked Juliet nervously.

"I think we'd better," said Jerome. "Dames like that, you don't want to cross 'em."

———

The palace gate, made of finely wrought silver, swung silently open as they approached.

They entered a room with walls so high the curved blue ceiling seemed like a sky. Enormous windows— tall, and without glass—looked out onto sweeping views. With a start Juliet realized that the window farthest to the left showed a snow-covered scene, while the one to the right opened onto high summer.

At the far side of the room, across the black marble floor and mounted on a three-tiered dais, was a throne of ebony and silver.

On the throne sat the hag they had met on the path. Yet she seemed to grow younger with each step they took in her direction, so that by the time they were standing before her, she was a woman in her prime. Tall and elegant, with auburn hair and dark eyes, she was dressed in a white garment that draped over one shoulder. A wide band of intricately worked silver adorned her upper left arm.

"Welcome, child," she said. Her deep, beautiful voice throbbed with power.

Juliet felt a desperate need to curtsy. Unfortunately, that seemed absurd for someone wearing jeans and a sweatshirt. Finally, she bowed her head in respect.

"Rise," said the woman, putting the tips of her fingers under Juliet's chin.

Juliet tingled at the touch, which was cool yet filled with strange power. "Wh—who are you?" she stammered.

"Like others you have met, I have been known by many names. For the story you are trapped in now, Hera is probably the most useful."

"You're the queen of the gods?" cried Juliet.

Hera smiled. "I was, at least some of the time." She shook her head. "We were very young when those stories were first lived. Young and foolish and careless of our power. Arrogant and sure we would go on forever . . ."

"You mean you won't? I thought you were immortal?"

Hera's smile was more rueful now. "It doesn't seem likely. Oh, we were *called* the immortals. We even believed it ourselves, for a while. And I suppose to humans anyone who lives for thousands of years would truly seem immortal. But there is an end in sight. Oh, yes. There is an end." She shook her head. "The great joke is that our lives seem to be divided out not unlike those of you humans. Which means it took us an awfully long time to grow up. Our adolescence lasted for centuries. And, like humans, we continue to pay the price for decisions we made in our youth, continue trying to straighten up the messes we created. And, alas, some of us—like my cousin Eris—have the very human trait of never managing to grow up at all."

"It was Eris who gave me this amulet," said Juliet, lifting her hand to her neck.

Hera nodded. "I was aware of this."

"Why?" asked Juliet. "And why me?"

"As to why: Eris wants the amulet back in the world, where it can work new mischief. As to why you: Well, as you humans are fond of saying, 'The gods move in mysterious ways.' However, I suspect the truth is that you just happened to be in the wrong place at the wrong time."

Juliet sighed. Cradling the amulet in her hand she asked, "What is this, exactly?"

"A prison."

Juliet touched the chain nervously. "Will I ever be able to take it off?"

"I hope so."

"What do I have to do?"

"Help the story come to its conclusion."

"What story?"

"The one you're trapped in."

"What story is that?"

Hera shook her head. "It's hard to say. In some ways stories are all the same and in other ways, even the old ones are always changing. This much I *can* tell you: You must follow it through to the end. No one gets out of the story they're in without doing that—at least not without paying a high price in regret and confusion." She leaned down and kissed Juliet on the brow. "This will help protect you. Now you must go. It is not good for you to spend too much time in this realm, and I suspect there are things you still must do here."

Her heart filled with a longing she did not understand, Juliet watched as Hera returned to her throne. Then, Roxanne and Jerome still clinging to her shoulders, Juliet turned to go. Suddenly it occurred to her that she needed to ask one more question. But when she turned back, the throne was gone, and the goddess with it.

"Now what do we do?" cried Juliet. "I was going to ask her how to get home!"

"I'd say the first thing we do is get outta here," replied Jerome. "This place gives me the creeps."

Juliet hurried on to the silver gate. As she stepped through, they heard a sighing sound behind them. Looking back, Juliet saw that the palace itself had vanished. Where it had stood, the path now continued on, clear and distinct.

"Okay," said Jerome. "I wasn't expecting that one!"

"Maybe we'd better start back now," said Roxanne.

But the path behind them, the path they had already followed, had vanished, too. The only way open to them was the path ahead, through where the palace had been. Juliet felt a moment of stomach-clenching fear.

"Do you think we'll ever get home?" she whispered.

"I'm pretty sure of it," said Roxanne calmly.

"What makes *you* so certain?" asked Jerome.

"Because whatever those goddesses are up to, they want it to happen in the real world. I mean, our world. So I figure they're going to make sure we get back."

"Huh," said Jerome. "That actually makes sense, Roxie."

Feeling slightly better, Juliet walked on.

The path continued to cling to the edge of the cliff, but the cliff itself was getting lower again. Eventually it dwindled to little more than a bluff. The path went down its side, leading them to a pebbled beach.

"Look!" said Roxanne. "Someone's coming!"

ELEVEN

Field of Gold

Walking toward them was a young woman—barely more than a girl, really—dressed all in rags. Her face was so filled with grief it made Juliet want to weep just to look at her.

"Who are you?" asked Juliet when the woman had drawn close enough to speak to her.

"My name has no meaning," she replied wearily.

"Well, you have to have a name," said Roxanne.

"Yeah," said Jerome. "Otherwise how can they call you to dinner?"

The trace of a smile curved the woman's lips for just a moment. Then she sighed and said, "No one calls me to dinner. I gather what I can along the path."

"Where are you going?" asked Juliet.

"Across the wood, through the word, around the world. I'll travel until I find my love, though it take me all my life." She chanted the words as if she had said them a thousand times already.

"What happened to him?" asked Juliet. "Your love, I mean."

The woman—beautiful enough to be a princess in a fairy tale, Juliet realized—stared out across the waves. Gulls were circling, cawing. A salty breeze teased through Juliet's coppery curls.

"I broke faith," the woman said at last. "I had been taken to his palace as part of a bargain between my father and his mother. At first I was furious and would have nothing to do with him—not that I needed to have much to do with him, for I never saw him. This was a relief, for I had been told he was a monster."

"Never saw him?" said Roxanne. "Sheesh, that's a heck of a love story."

"Hey, if you never see someone, you can't fight with them," said Jerome.

"Oh, we fought! The reason I never saw him was that he came to me only in darkness. He would sit near me and talk in a voice so sweet and soft and filled with kindness that little by little my rage began to fade. In time I no longer worried whether he was monster or man. We fell in love, and accepted each other as husband and wife. But he was steadfast in his rule that I must never see him, and I freely promised to honor him in this wish."

She shook her head. Her tears were flowing freely now. "I did not keep my promise. My desire to see my beloved, even if he was monstrous and malformed, grew stronger and stronger. Finally, one night I slipped from our bed and fetched a lamp, thinking to shine a light on him for the merest instant. But when the light fell on his face, I cried out and my hand shook."

"Because he was so ugly?" asked Jerome eagerly.

"Because he was so beautiful," said the woman with a sigh.

"Men," said Roxanne.

"In the moment that my hand shook, a drop of the lamp's hot oil fell on my husband's shoulder. He sprang to his feet with a cry of pain—pain that quickly turned to horror when he realized what I had done. I blew out the lamp at once. But it was too late. He was gone and all that was left were his grief-stricken last words, which hung in the air like a lash to my heart. 'My love, my love, why could you not be true to your promise?' "

"That's horrible," sniffed Roxanne, tiny tears rolling down her whiskers.

"What happened next?" asked Juliet breathlessly.

The girl sighed. "His mother came to me. She was as beautiful as a statue, and just as cold, just as hard. She scolded me for breaking my promise, and when I wept and asked what I must do to regain my love, she told me I could wander in this world and out of it, but I would never find my love until the mouse had roared."

Juliet shivered. That weird poem Mr. Suss had recited also said the mouse must roar. What was going on here?

"Man, that's a tough one," said Jerome. "I mean, we're *rats*, and we can't roar. So what's a little mouse gonna do?"

"I don't know," said the woman. "But I will not stop looking. Even so—" She paused and looked around, seeming a bit confused.

"What is it?" asked Juliet.

The woman shook her head. "It's odd. I feel as if I've been asleep for a long time and have just awoken again."

"I wish there was something I could do for you," said Juliet softly.

The woman started to reply, then gasped and pointed to Juliet's chest.

Juliet glanced down. Though she had tucked the amulet under her sweatshirt, it was now glowing so brightly that light shone right through the fabric. Instinctively, she put her fingers over the light to hide it. The spot was warm, though not unpleasantly so. Yet she was so frightened that she longed to rip the amulet from her neck and fling it away. Except, of course, she couldn't.

The young woman reached forward in awe. "What is that?"

Reluctantly Juliet pulled out the amulet.

The woman's fingers trembled as she reached toward it. "I feel something strange about this, as if it is important to me in some way. What may I do to earn it from you?"

"I'd *give* it to you if I could!" said Juliet. "But the chain is too small. I can't take it off."

"Ah," said the woman, nodding. "So you are also under a burden of enchantment. Do you have a task you must accomplish?"

"I'm supposed to find the key that will unlock this amulet. But even if I could find the key, I don't know if I would dare to use it. I'm afraid of what might be inside."

"The tasks given by the gods are often fearful. The only thing more fearful is what happens if you turn away from them."

"You're saying that if I manage to find the key, I had better open the amulet, right?"

"I cannot imagine otherwise."

Juliet sighed. "Right now I just want to go home. I don't think I belong in this world."

The woman nodded. "I could tell you were from the other side. Well, at least I can help you with that matter." Pointing to a spot not far ahead of them she said, "When you come to the place where the path divides, go left. In time you will come to a field of golden flowers. On the far side of the field, you will find an ancient oak that has been split by lightning. Step between the two halves of its trunk, and I believe you will find your way home." The woman put a hand on Juliet's cheek. "Good luck," she said. "I hope we may meet again." With a final glance at the amulet, she turned and walked along the beach. She had not gone more than ten steps when the mist closed around her and she vanished.

"Well, there goes another one!" said Roxanne.

"I wish I could help her," said Juliet.

"We've got enough to do to help ourselves right now," said Jerome. "Come on, let's get going."

Juliet started in the direction the woman had indicated. Soon enough they came to the place where the path split.

"Go left," said Jerome.

"I *know* that," replied Juliet.

"There it is!" cried Roxanne a moment later. "The field of flowers."

Indeed, opening ahead of them was a broad meadow, filled with beautiful yellow flowers. It looked oddly familiar to Juliet, though at first she could not say why. But as they started across, it came clear to her. "This is the same meadow that's in my attic!" she cried.

"Oh, brother," said Jerome. "The kid has finally cracked."

"Must be the pressure was too much for her," said Roxanne sadly.

"You talk to her, Roxie. You're better at this stuff than I am."

"Don't be silly!" said Juliet. "I'm perfectly fine. I don't mean there's an actual field in my attic. But there's a painting of this field. I was looking at it just before you showed up yesterday."

"Are you sure?" asked Roxanne.

"Positive. I wonder if . . . no, that's silly. It wouldn't be possible."

Jerome snorted impatiently. "You just had a talk with the queen of the gods, then met some dame who seems trapped in a fairy tale, and now you're crossing a meadow that you've got a painting of in your attic, carrying a pair of talking rats on your shoulders, and you think something is impossible? Geez, Juliet, I don't think you been paying close enough attention."

Juliet sighed. "I just had a silly thought was all. There's a boy in the painting and . . . good grief! There he is!"

The rats looked in the direction Juliet was pointing. A young boy—he looked no older than Byron—

was standing on a pile of rocks, scanning the horizon. He looked scared, and sad.

Juliet hurried over to him. "What's wrong?" she asked.

"Who are you?" cried the boy. He looked startled, and a little frightened.

He's got a right to be startled, thought Juliet when she realized how strange her clothing must appear to him—not to mention the fact that she had a rat on each shoulder.

"I'm just a traveler," she said gently. "But you looked upset, and I wondered if we could help."

"I've lost one of the small ones," sniffed the boy. "It's wandered off. I can't leave the flock to look for it."

"Maybe we can find it for you," said Juliet. "Which way did it go?"

"Why would you want to help me?" asked the boy.

"Good question," said Jerome. "We do need to get back to our own side, Juliet."

And then it came to her, the idea that had been nagging at the back of her mind since they first reached the meadow. "Because it's how we're going to find the key to the amulet!"

"What are you talking about?" asked Jerome.

"It's the poem, the one Terry Suss told me on the playground the other day.

> "Past field of gold,
> The key is hid.
> Ignore the child,
> And find the kid!"

"At first I thought it was just some sort of joke. How could you ignore the child and find the kid? But now I understand—the kid is the baby goat. And look at all these flowers. *This* is the field of gold. I should have figured it out sooner. We have to go find that kid!"

"Maybe we should split up," said Roxanne.

"I dunno," said Jerome. "The way things are around here, I'm afraid if we do, one of us could end up somewhere else altogether. We might never find each other again."

"Yeah, I guess you're right. Okay, let's do it this way. Put us down, Juliet. You stay here, and me and Jerome will go check with some of the other animals."

Juliet scowled. "What do you mean, check with the other animals?"

Roxanne shrugged. "We'll just ask them if they know where the kid went."

"You can talk to animals?"

"Yeah," said Jerome. "Generally we don't bother, on account of most of them ain't very cultured. I did meet this sweet little rat in a museum once, but..." His voice faltered, and he glanced at Roxanne, who had crossed her arms and was looking in the other direction. "But that was a big mistake," he finished lamely.

"If you're quite finished," said Roxanne, her voice icy, "let's go do some work."

Juliet watched the two rats scamper off among the flowers. She suddenly felt very alone. She would have liked to talk to the goatherd, but she was too shy to speak first, and he appeared totally terrified by her presence. She brushed off a rock and sat down to wait in silence. As time went on, she began to wish she had brought her watch. How long had Roxanne and Jerome been gone? Just as Juliet felt the stirrings of panic, something rustled in the flowers at her feet. Looking down, she saw Roxanne.

"We found him!" said the rat. "You'd better come along. Bring the boy, too."

"Why?"

" 'Cause he's stuck in a cave, and we can't get him out on our own. You're going to have to move a rock, and it's pretty big."

Juliet went to the boy. "My friends have found your lost kid," she said. "He's stuck in a cave. If you come with me, we might be able to free him."

The boy stared at Juliet for a moment, his dark eyes wide. "You are very beautiful," he said at last. "I will follow you anywhere."

Juliet sighed. Then, reminding herself that the boy was just another victim of the amulet, she said, "Thank you. Now let's go get your goat."

As they followed Roxanne across the field of golden flowers, Juliet felt a great sense of rightness. The world was beautiful, and she was in the right place, doing the right thing. She had never experienced such a feeling of peace.

But when they came to the stony hill that rose at the far side of the field and Roxanne stood on her hind legs and pointed at the dark mouth of a cave and said, "In there," Juliet's feeling of serenity vanished.

Well, at least she had the flashlight—though when she turned it on, the boy cried out and stepped fearfully back from her.

"It's all right," she said gently. "Light is a gift from the gods."

The boy smiled, and followed her into the cave.

"Back here!" called Jerome when he saw the light. "It's back here!"

They picked their way over the stony floor, bending low, for the cave was no more than four feet high. Jerome was standing next to the young goat, which had caught its leg in the space between the rock and the cave wall.

"Oh, foolish kid," murmured the boy tenderly. "What brought you to such a place?"

He bent to move the rock but could not budge it. Juliet put down the flashlight and bent to help. Heaving and pushing together, they managed to shift it slightly—enough so that the kid, with a "maaaa" of relief, could pull itself free.

The goatherd gathered the stray in his arms. As he did, Juliet caught her breath. Where the rock had been, shining in the beam of her flashlight, was a tiny key.

She knelt to pick it up.

The instant her fingers touched it, the world began to dissolve around her. She heard the boy cry out—and then there was nothing but silence, and blackness.

TWELVE

Prisoner of Love

Juliet's heart was pounding. "Roxanne?" she whispered. "Jerome? Are you still with me?"

"We're here," answered the rats together.

Juliet flicked on the flashlight and yelped in surprise. She was standing in the attic of her own house! And right in front of her was the painting she had looked at so many times, the one Great Aunt Bessie had brought home from Greece—the painting of a field of golden flowers with its young shepherd. But the picture had changed. Though the youth was still looking out over his flock, in his arms he now held a spindly legged kid, and on his face was an expression of pride and relief.

Juliet wasn't sure whether she found the change in the painting delightful, or terrifying.

"Wowza," said Jerome. "That was one weird trip— even for us!"

"Be quiet," cautioned Juliet. "I don't want anyone to hear us while we're going down to my room."

"Won't they all be asleep?" asked Roxanne.

"I don't know. I don't know what time it is. My father might be up by now."

"Already?" asked Jerome. He glanced toward the window at the end of the attic. "It's still dark!"

"Dad's an early riser. He says the dawn delights and inspires him." She didn't add that he had been getting up early lately because he was so worried about the poetry festival. "And my mother gets up even earlier sometimes. She likes to work in the middle of the night. She says it's easier to concentrate."

"You've got sort of an odd family," said Roxanne.

"Yeah, too bad we're not normal—like talking rats!"

"Geez," said Jerome. "No need to get touchy!"

Walking softly, guided by her flashlight, Juliet crossed the attic and peered out. The door to her mother's studio was open, but the room was dark. Feeling a little calmer, she started down the stairs. At the bottom she put her hand over the flashlight, so only a little light leaked out around the edges. Then she tiptoed to her room. She was barely through the door when a voice said, "There you are! I was starting to get worried."

It was all Juliet could do to keep from screaming. "Byron!" she hissed. "What are you doing here? You scared me half to death!"

"I've been waiting for you! I wanted to find out what happened."

"How long have you been here?" She paused, then added, "What time is it, anyway?"

Her brother shrugged. "About quarter past one."

"That can't be right! We were gone for hours."

"It's right. I set my alarm for half past midnight so I would be up when you got back."

"But how—"

"Don't think about it," advised Jerome. "We've got other things to deal with right now."

"Right," said Roxanne. "It's time to use that key!"

"What key?" asked Byron.

He listened eagerly as Juliet and the rats filled him in on what had happened while they were in the other realm. When they finished, he said bitterly, "Oh, man, I can't believe I didn't get to go. Okay, what about the key? Now that you've got it, are you really going to open the amulet?"

"I think I have to," said Juliet. She slipped her finger between the chain and her neck. "At least this doesn't seem to be getting any tighter. I wonder if I could break it if I yanked hard enough."

"More likely you'd just hurt your neck," said Roxanne.

"But feel free to give it a try," added Jerome. "It'd be kind of interesting to see if you can yank it hard enough to cut off your own head."

"Be nice, Jerome!" said Roxanne.

"Thing is, I'd really like to take it off before I use this key," Juliet said.

"I don't think that's gonna happen," said Jerome. "Better just use the key and get it over with."

Juliet took the key, which was no longer than her fingernail, and inserted it in the tiny lock. She turned it and heard a tiny click. The amulet swung open. A rush of air—warm, sweet, and musky smelling—brushed past her cheek.

Then a man's finger thrust straight out from the amulet.

Byron leaped back with a cry of fear. Juliet wanted to scream, too, but was so terrified, she couldn't make a sound. She clawed at the chain, but it was unbreakable.

The finger moved around as if trying to find something to touch. Juliet tipped her head back as far as she could, her eyes wide with fright.

"Jerome," whispered Roxanne. "What the heck is going on here?"

"I dunno, Roxie. But whatever it is, I don't like it!"

The finger touched Juliet's chin. She gasped in horror and dropped the amulet. At the same time, the finger withdrew, as if it had been burned.

Before Juliet could catch her breath, a male voice, rich and beautiful, asked plaintively, *Who are you?*

Juliet looked around, then realized that the words had not been spoken out loud, but instead had formed directly in her mind. Terrified, she clutched the sides of her head.

"Who are *you?*" she squeaked. "And how did you do that?"

"Who are you talking to?" asked Byron.

Juliet waved a hand to silence her brother as the voice in her head said, *I am the prisoner of the amulet. I was hoping someone might open it soon. I've been aching to talk to you! I need your help.*

"*My* help?" asked Juliet, still speaking out loud.

To free me.

Juliet's heart hammered against her ribs, and she wanted nothing more than to fling the amulet out the window. But it was held tight about her neck by the magic chain.

"Who are you?" she whispered again.

Jerome scurried over. Tugging on her sleeve, he asked urgently, "Juliet, what's going on? Who are you talking to?"

"Shhh! Let me listen!"

Certainly you must have heard of me, said the voice, sounding almost mournful. *Or has the world turned completely away from the god of love?*

"The *god* of love?" asked Juliet. "I know there's a *goddess* of love. Aphrodite, she's called. Or sometimes Venus."

That's my mother!

"Then who are you?"

Do you mean you've never heard of Eros—or perhaps you know me as Cupid?

"*Cupid?*" Juliet asked in astonishment. "You're Cupid?"

"You're talking to *Cupid?*" echoed Byron.

Juliet put her hands on her hips. "If you're Cupid, what are you doing inside this amulet?"

I told you: It is my prison.

"Juliet!" shouted Jerome. "What the heck is going on here?"

"Just a moment," said Juliet to the amulet. Turning to the rats and Byron, she said, "Whoever is in the amulet is talking directly into my head. He claims that he's Cupid."

"Good grief," said Jerome. Flinging himself to his stomach, he muttered, "Maybe if I'd had a mother, she could have warned me about days like this."

"Be quiet," said Roxanne. "Let Juliet talk to him. Maybe we'll finally get somewhere."

"Would it be possible for you to talk out loud?" asked Juliet. "It might make things easier."

Give me a moment. It's been a long time since I actually used my voice.

"He's working on it," whispered Juliet to the others.

"How's this?" asked Cupid.

The words, spoken out loud, came directly from the amulet, causing Byron, Jerome, and Roxanne to cry out in surprise.

"Much better," said Juliet. "Thank you."

"You're welcome."

"I'm confused about something. You called the amulet your prison. But you couldn't possibly fit inside this tiny thing. Heck, if you were inside it, I couldn't even lift it!"

"Do not underestimate the powers of the old ones. The amulet is bigger on the inside than it is on the outside. It holds me easily. My prison is comfortable enough. Even so, freedom would be better." He paused, then said, "I think this would be easier if we had a chance to see each other."

"How can we do that?"

"Are you near a mirror?"

"There's one right in front of me."

"Then just point the amulet right at it."

Juliet did as the voice asked. Looking directly at herself, she could see the open pendant dangling around her neck.

Suddenly an eye appeared at the opening.

Juliet squeaked in fright.

"Oh, hush! I told you, I just want to see you. You're a very lovely girl. I like the green eyes. It's a nice touch. Now, if you want to see me, lift the amulet and peek in."

Juliet started to raise the amulet, then said, "Won't this put you upside down?"

The voice actually laughed. "No. The opening is just a hole in the wall of my cell. It moves around as you move the amulet."

Juliet tried to lift the amulet to her eye but gave up in frustration. "I can't do it. The chain's too short!"

"I can look in it for you!" said Roxanne. She scurried over to the desk. Standing on her hind legs, she put one eye to the amulet.

"What do you see?" asked Juliet eagerly.

"Oooh, he's handsome! But he doesn't have much on. Maybe it's just as well you can't see him."

"Are you telling me he's naked?" asked Juliet, horrified at the idea that she was wearing a naked man around her neck.

"Well, he's not quite naked. He's got this piece of white cloth that goes over his shoulder and around his waist. Big gray eyes. Curly golden hair. Oh, and wings. Big white ones, almost as tall as he is. Also, he's got a bow and arrow."

"What does his cell look like?"

"Not much to it. Sort of like the inside of an egg, just kind of white and rounded."

Juliet shuddered, thinking how horrible it must be to be trapped in a space like that. "Who locked you in there?" she asked Cupid.

"My mother."

"Are you kidding? Why would your mother do a thing like that?"

"She did it in a fit of anger. Mother is the jealous sort, which is one of the problems with romantic love. When she was angry, she didn't always think about what she was doing. Putting me in this amulet, for example, made it a very dangerous item. After Mother gave it to Helen—"

"Helen of Troy?" gasped Juliet.

"Who else?"

"Was she really the most beautiful woman in the world?" asked Byron eagerly.

Cupid snorted. "She was pretty enough. But not so pretty that she could have caused that horrible war all by herself. I had a lot to do with it."

"You *wanted* the Trojan War to happen?" asked Juliet, aghast.

"Don't be silly. I simply mean I had a lot to do with the war because as long as Helen was wearing me around her neck, she was so irresistible that men were willing to die for her."

Juliet shuddered. "That's not going to happen to me, is it?" she demanded.

"Not right away. I'm just waking up again. It will

take some time for my power to return to full strength. It's very confusing right now. It's as if there was a long period of . . . nothing. I wonder if the gods have gone to sleep. But not long ago, I was pulled from my slumber. My heart still stings with love and loss, and I am mightily weary of this prison, which I beg you to release me from."

"If I do release you, are you going to run around making people fall in love with each other?" asked Juliet.

"I can't deny that when I'm around humans, I do feel that urge. But I am much more interested in finding Psyche."

"Who's Psyche?"

"The woman I love. She's the reason Mother imprisoned me in this amulet."

"I don't understand," said Juliet.

Cupid was silent for a moment. Finally he said, "As I told you, Mother is the jealous sort. So she got very upset when she learned there was a mortal girl who was so beautiful many men had turned their hearts toward her, claiming she was like the goddess of love on Earth. In her fury, she sent me to teach the girl a lesson."

"What kind of a lesson?"

"I was supposed to make Psyche fall in love with a monster. Which, of course, I could easily do with my magical arrows of love. The problem was, Psyche really was as beautiful as everyone said, and I fell in love with her myself—partly because I was so startled by her beauty that I scratched myself with the arrow I had meant to shoot at her. To make a long story short, I took her for my bride. I couldn't tell mother this, of course, so I put out a story that Psyche's father had forced her to marry a monster, which made Mother very happy. Then I put Psyche in a palace, hoping that in time I could bring Mother to accept her."

Cupid sighed. "Unfortunately, Mother was not much given to changing her mind—or forgiving anyone she felt had crossed her. And because I could not allow Psyche to see me until Mother accepted our marriage, I visited her only under cover of darkness. Even then I continued to pretend I was a monster, so Mother would not learn of what I was doing. But in those visits, in the quiet darkness, hidden by night's inky cloak, Psyche and I spoke of love. In time she no longer worried whether I was man or monster— never suspecting that I was a god—and came to love me truly. We had the deepest and best of loves, the love that contains both eros and *agapé,* and we became man and wife in fact as well as name. But still I could not let my beloved see me, and I was always gone before rosy-fingered dawn arrived."

Cupid was silent for a while. Finally he said, "Perhaps to never see her husband was a harder thing than I should have asked Psyche to bear. One night the temptation became too much. After I had fallen asleep, she slipped from our bed to fetch a lamp so she could catch a glimpse of me. But her hand trembled and hot oil fell on my shoulder. In that moment Mother's wrath was ignited. Spells were cast. I was flung into this prison, and my dearest love was set to endless wandering."

A chill ran along Juliet's spine. "We just met a woman who told us the same story," she said. "It must have been Psyche!"

"What are you saying?" cried Cupid.

Juliet told him about the evening's journey, and all that she and the rats had experienced. "But I don't understand," she said, as she finished her story. "How can Psyche still be alive? Didn't this all happen a long, long time ago?"

"Very long ago," said Cupid sadly. "There are mysteries here that must be unraveled. You *must* release me from this prison!"

"I'd be glad to! But I don't know how!"

"No one has told you anything in your travels?"

Juliet took a deep breath. "No, they have told me some things. I'm supposed to find a mouse that can roar. But I don't have any idea how the heck I'm supposed to do *that*!"

"Well, if you don't want to be carrying me around your neck for the rest of your life, you're going to have to try. But at least I can help you now. I must warn you about something, though."

"Now what?" said Jerome. "I'll tell ya, Elives is gonna owe us one heck of a bonus before this is over!"

"While I was sleeping, the amulet's power was dormant, drowsing much as I was. Now that I am awake, its power will begin to spread, casting a spell of love that no man will be able to resist."

"What are you saying?" cried Juliet.

"Before long you will have more adoration coming toward you than you can imagine."

"Juliet Dove, Queen of Love!" said Byron in awe.

Juliet was stunned by the idea. "That's like my worst nightmare," she whispered. Suddenly an even more appalling thought struck her. "Cupid, if you make *me* fall in love with anyone, I swear I'll throw this amulet in the ocean! Unless someone drags you up from the bottom of the sea, you'll never get out of it. So don't mess with me!"

"Calm down, Juliet," said Cupid gently. Then, with a hint of a laugh in his voice, he added, "Besides, I'm not sure how you'd throw me in the ocean without coming along yourself."

"He's got you there, Juliet," said Jerome.

"For the time being," continued Cupid, "whatever we do, we will have to do together. I do not want to cause you problems, Juliet, but I cannot help being what I am. I do not know what forces framed me, nor for what reason I was brought into being. That is as much a mystery to the gods as it is to you humans. But I do know that wherever I go, love swirls like a storm, and chaos often follows. The sooner you can find a way to free me, the better for both of us. I ache to find my own lost love and hold her in my arms once again. In truth, I am a prisoner of love myself—my body held here, my heart held by Psyche."

The sorrow in his voice pricked Juliet's conscience. "Of course I'll try to help you. But can't you do anything to get the boys to leave me alone?"

"Truly, it is much easier to turn that kind of thing *on* than it is to turn it *off*."

"Well I'm not going to be able to help you if I'm constantly fighting off a pack of boys."

"Yet the only way you're going to be free of that pack of boys is by helping me! Once you release me from this prison, the magic that binds the chain around your neck will be broken. But until I *do* get out of here, things are only going to get worse as far as the boy situation is concerned, and there's not a thing I can do about it. I told you, now that I'm awake, my power will grow stronger by the hour."

Juliet turned to Roxanne and Jerome. "I think you'd better go tell Mr. Elives what's happening."

"Good idea," said Roxanne.

"I'm on my way," said Jerome. He stood on his hind legs, gave Juliet a little salute, then scuttled under the bed and disappeared.

As they waited for Jerome to return, Cupid told Juliet stories about life among the gods. She felt almost as if she had been swept back to the days of Mount Olympus. Cupid was well into the tale of Demeter and Persephone when Jerome bolted from beneath the bed and gasped, "Bad news! Really, *really* bad news!"

"What is it?" cried Roxanne. "What's happened?"

"I can't find the magic shop!"

"What do you mean you can't find it? It doesn't make any difference where it is; we always just go back to it."

"Not this time we don't. It's missing! I been wandering around . . . well, I don't know where. But it was pretty scary. Finally, I decided to come back here before I got totally lost."

"Eris must have done something," said Juliet.

"Eris?" asked Cupid in alarm.

"We think she's the one who gave me the amulet to begin with."

"This is not good news. If Eris has her hand in this, trouble is sure to follow."

But though they talked for another hour, none of them could think of what to do next. Finally, yawning broadly, Byron shuffled off to his own room. Juliet, too exhausted to stay awake, closed the amulet and fell into a fitful sleep filled with dreams in which boys with the heads of rats chased her down the street, trying to kiss her.

When she awoke, she found Roxanne and Jerome sleeping next to her on her pillow. "Good grief!" she cried in astonishment. "What happened to you two?"

THIRTEEN

Cupid's Little Helpers

Jerome stretched and yawned. "Sheesh, couldn't you wake a guy up a little more gently?" he complained, not even opening his eyes. "I was having this great dream about—"

"Jerome," interrupted Juliet. "You've...you've got wings!"

The rat opened one eye. "What are you talking about?" he asked drowsily. Then he looked across the pillow and sprang to his feet. "Roxanne! She's not kidding. You've got wings!"

Roxanne was on her hind legs now, staring wildly at Jerome. "So do you!" she cried. "So do you!"

Indeed, during the night both rats had sprouted wings. Not bat wings, as might have been expected for a pair of rodents. These wings were small, white, and feathery. They looked like something you might see on a Valentine's Day card made for a rat.

"Hey!" cried Roxanne as she fluttered her wings and lifted a couple of inches off the pillow. "They work!" Delight and fear seemed to chase each other across her face. "I'm flying!"

A moment later Jerome was in the air as well. Soon the two rats were flitting about the room, laughing merrily as they discovered the joys of flight.

"Stop!" cried Juliet. "We've got to figure out what's going on here!"

That's easy enough, said Cupid, speaking directly into her mind. *I told you my powers would be rising now that I am awake. I'm afraid this is my fault.*

"Why aren't you talking out loud?" asked Juliet, clutching the sides of her head again.

Because you closed the amulet. Besides, I thought it would be easier if you and I could talk about certain things without the rats listening in. Why don't you try to answer me back the same way? It shouldn't be hard.

"But I don't want you in my head!"

You may before the day is over!

"Let's deal with one thing at a time," said Juliet. She opened the amulet so Cupid could speak out loud, then said, "Did you really do this to Roxanne and Jerome?"

"Not on purpose," came the voice from the amulet. "In fact, I had no idea it was happening until I heard you shouting. Even so, it does seem likely that their metamorphosis is a result of my power seeking a way to be free in the world. Until I can be loosed from the amulet, Roxanne and Jerome will be representing me."

Suddenly Juliet noticed a tiny harp laying on her pillow, right where Roxanne had been sleeping. As she watched, a miniature bow took shape in the spot where Jerome had been. She hesitated to mention these things to the rats. She didn't need to. They came swooping back as if they sensed that the items had appeared.

"Presents!" cried Roxanne. Snatching up the harp, she ran her claws over it. A cascade of beautiful music poured out. Juliet felt a swelling in her heart, as if she were filled with a deep, all encompassing love that had nowhere to go.

Meanwhile Jerome was hovering over his place on the pillow. "A bow and arrow!" he cried happily. "I always wanted one of them!"

"Don't you dare shoot me with that thing!" commanded Juliet.

"Aw, I wouldn't shoot *you*, Juliet," said Jerome. Then, sounding disappointed, he said, "Besides, I've only got one arrow. I'd better save it for when I really need it."

You may tell him there will be as many arrows as he needs, said Cupid, speaking directly into Juliet's mind once more. *Each time he lets fly an arrow, another will take its place. It's part of the magic of the bow.*

"I'm not sure I want him to know that," muttered Juliet.

"Know what?" asked Jerome.

She sighed. "You'll have as many arrows as you need. They replace themselves magically."

"Wowza! This is going to be fun!"

"You'd better be careful," warned Juliet. "It could also be dangerous."

"What could be dangerous?" asked Roxanne, doing a backward somersault two feet above Juliet's dresser. "We're Cupid's little helpers, spreading love wherever we go!"

"That's what's so dangerous!" cried Juliet. "Love is nothing to mess around with!"

I fear this is going to be a difficult day, said Cupid, still speaking to her directly. *I think—*

His words were cut off by a voice at the door.

"Juliet, what the heck is going on in here?"

It was Margaret. She was just outside Juliet's room, holding the sluggarium. Her hair this morning was flame red. Juliet waited for her sister to scream at the sight of the flying rats, but Margaret just stood there, gazing at Juliet with a puzzled expression. "I heard you reciting. Are you going to do a poem at the jam after all? That would sure make Dad happy."

Juliet looked for Roxanne and Jerome. They were hovering near the head of her bed. Didn't Margaret see them?

"I'm . . . trying to work out something I have to do for school," said Juliet. This was close to the truth, since she was going to have to go to school in about an hour, and she was fairly sure Roxanne and Jerome would be going with her.

Roxanne fluttered across the room. Hanging in the air just above Margaret's head, she strummed her harp. Beautiful music flowed out. Though it was clear to Juliet that her sister could not actually hear the notes, Margaret's face softened. With a gentle smile, she said, "Well, if you want help reading lines or any-

thing, just let me know. I'll be glad to work with you."
She looked down at the sluggarium. "Come on, kids.
Time for your morning bath!"

As soon as Margaret was gone, Juliet closed her
door. Speaking more softly than she had before, she
said, "Cupid! How come Margaret couldn't see
Jerome and Roxanne?"

"I'm sure you've heard the saying that love is
blind," replied Cupid. "That got started partly because those of us who specialize in it are often invisible."

Juliet looked at the pair of winged rats—invisible
winged rats who were carriers of irresistible love—
and put her hand over the amulet. "How did I get myself into this?" she muttered.

Cupid did not answer.

Byron came to her door next. "Where's Roxanne
and Jerome?" he asked, looking around.

"You mean you can't see them, either?" asked
Juliet.

He shook his head, looking puzzled then astonished as Juliet explained the latest development.
When she was done, he stared around the room and
said, "Hey, Jerome and Roxanne, I wish I could still
see you!"

"They're here," said Juliet, gesturing with her
thumbs. "Just over my shoulders." She listened for a
second, then said, "Roxanne says to tell you that
you're a very nice boy, and she hopes you don't think
it's rude of her to be invisible."

———

Because the kitchen floor remained a work in progress, the Doves ate breakfast in the dining room. Jerome and Roxanne hovered in a corner. Juliet could tell that Jerome was longing to use his bow and arrow, but there were no good targets—until Queen Baboo de la Roo came strolling into the room.

"Oh, look," said Mr. Dove. "It's the furry land whale!"

The cat waddled over to Margaret to beg for a tidbit—a habit that distressed Mr. Dove no end—then went to sit under the buffet. Jerome and Roxanne, clearly enjoying the fact that they were invisible to everyone but Juliet, fluttered down for a closer look at the feline.

At that moment a mouse came scurrying along the wall.

Queen Baboo started up. Juliet was tempted to go after the mouse herself, in the desperate hope that she might be able to teach it to roar. She held herself back. Queen Baboo, of course, had no such sense of restraint. But just as the cat was about to lunge for the little creature, Jerome loosed his love arrow. The tiny dart disappeared in Queen Baboo's shaggy gray fur. Instantly the cat stopped, flopped onto her side, and began to purr.

The mouse scuttled into a hole in the wall.

Queen Baboo stared after it longingly. Patting at the wall with her paw, she let out a heartbroken "Miao!"

It was about the most pathetic sound Juliet had ever heard.

"Score one for the rodents!" cried Jerome, doing a little victory dance in midair.

Juliet noticed that his bow already had another arrow in it.

When it was time to leave for school, Juliet decided to go out the front way, rather than crossing the backyard to walk with Arturo. As she opened the door to leave, she saw three bouquets on the front steps. Rolling her eyes she scooped them up and carried them to the trash can, pointedly not looking at the notes that said who they were from.

"What did you do that for?" asked Roxanne, who was hovering just above Juliet's left shoulder. "They were pretty!"

"Because I don't want to encourage anyone," said Juliet grimly.

"Encouraging people is nice."

"Not when the cause is hopeless," growled Juliet.

Henry Patterson, the third grader from down the street, was waiting for her at the corner.

"Hi, Juliet," he said shyly.

"Hi, Henry," she replied, relieved to talk to a male who wasn't in love with her. At least she thought that was the case, until Henry held out a Snickers bar and said adoringly, "I got this for you."

Juliet had an urge to grab the candy and stomp on it. But Henry was so cute that she couldn't bring herself to do that, so she just said, "Thank you, Henry, that was very nice of you," and tucked the gift into her backpack.

"I wish I could go to school with you," called Henry as Juliet started to walk away. Looking over her shoulder, she saw a tear trickling down his cheek.

"Did you shoot that poor little kid with one of those stupid arrows?" she muttered to Jerome once they were a few yards away.

"Are you kidding? That would have been a complete waste of a perfectly good arrow. You've already got all the love power you need. *More* than you need!"

"Can't you *do* anything about this, Cupid?" she whispered, grabbing the amulet.

I am what I am, replied the love god. *As long as I'm in the amulet, and as long as it is locked around your neck, you will command this kind of attention. The sooner you can get me out, the better, at least if ending the attention is what you really want.*

Little as she liked the idea, Juliet decided this was the time to try speaking to him mind to mind. *It's what I want!* she thought fiercely.

Good. Then we'll try to figure out how to find a mouse that can roar. In the meantime I'll try as best I can to keep my effects under control. You'd better do the same thing for the rats!

Believe me, I have no control over what those two do.

The mental conversation was interrupted by a shout from Jerome, who was fluttering somewhere to Juliet's right. "Yahoo!" he cried. "Direct hit!"

Juliet turned and was appalled to see the mailman chasing Henry's mother down the street.

"Jerome!" said Juliet fiercely. "You stop that right this instant!"

He grinned. "Sorry. Just wanted to see how it works on humans!"

By the time Juliet got to school, she had a trail of nearly two dozen boys behind her. She was doing her best to ignore them, but as she walked down the hall, she realized that the female portion of the student body was giving her a lot of nasty glances. More than once she saw clusters of girls whispering together. They would break apart when they noticed her approaching and pretend that nothing was going on, but Juliet was sure they were talking about her.

"What the heck is going on with the boys?" asked Elizabeth, just before they went into class. "Did you find some secret love potion on the Internet?"

Before Juliet could answer—and she had no idea what to say, anyway—Bambi and Samantha walked by. Glancing at Juliet, Samantha sneered, "Well, Killer, you must be giving the boys everything they want!"

This idea was so absurd that Juliet almost laughed—until she realized that Samantha actually meant it.

"What does she think I'm doing?" she asked Elizabeth.

"What *are* you doing?" replied Elizabeth.

Juliet's heart began to pound. "Do people think I'm, like, kissing the boys or something?"

Elizabeth shrugged. "All I know is that all the guys want to be near you all of a sudden."

Juliet noticed an odd tone in her friend's voice and suddenly wondered if Elizabeth might be jealous.

More than ever she wished she could explain about the amulet. It was sure nothing to be jealous about! Before Juliet could think of what to say, Elizabeth grabbed Juliet's arm and whispered. "Findley alert! Pete's heading this way!"

Juliet's cheeks flamed red. Pete Findley was an eighth grader who was both smart and handsome, and she had more than once had embarrassing daydreams about him. Her heart began to pound as he came over to lean beside her locker.

"Hey, Juliet," he said. "I hear you're having problems with that little snot, Bambi."

Juliet nodded, hardly able to imagine that Pete Findley would know, much less care, about what was going on in sixth grade.

"You just tell me if she bothers you too much," said Pete, reaching out to brush back a lock of her hair. Juliet dodged his hand, mentally kicking herself even as she did. Pete looked embarrassed, which made her feel even worse. "Sorry," he muttered.

He turned to Elizabeth. "Hey, your brother told me—"

He stopped in midsentence, then put his hand to his neck.

"Got him!" crowed Jerome.

Juliet glanced over at the rat, who was fluttering just above her shoulder. He had his little bow in hand. The string was still quivering and a new arrow appeared even as she watched. She turned back toward Pete. Roxanne was about two feet above his head, strumming her harp. A soft expression came over

Pete's face. "Gosh, Elizabeth," he said. "I...I never noticed how...gosh!"

Then he turned and fled.

Elizabeth stared after him in wonder. "What was *that* all about?"

Juliet shook her head. "Boys," was all she could say. She turned to glare at Jerome, then realized she would look as if she were staring at nothing. If she started doing *that,* people would really think she was crazy. But she couldn't believe he had just made the one boy she *did* want to notice her fall in love with Elizabeth.

How unfair could life get?

"Ain't love beautiful?" sighed Roxanne.

Juliet didn't answer.

The bell rang. Juliet and Elizabeth headed into their room, where a clump of boys instantly gathered around Juliet's desk, clamoring for her attention.

"All right, all right, let's break this up," said Ms. Spradling. "We've got work to do here."

But not much work got done that day, as the room was filled with sighs from the boys and angry glares from the girls. Shortly after lunch Juliet told Ms. Spradling she had a headache—which was not far from the truth—and asked if she could go to the nurse's office. Then she got the nurse to call her mother to pick her up.

She figured it was the only way to get home safely.

Given her preference, Juliet would have spent the entire night in her room. But by the time her mother called them to supper, hunger drove her to rejoin the family. She did manage to talk Roxanne and Jerome into staying upstairs.

"Sure," said Jerome. "I could use a nap, anyway. All that making people fall in love takes it out of a guy."

Juliet pulled one of her dresser drawers open a few inches. Now that they could not be seen by normal eyes, the rats didn't need to hide anymore. But the T-shirts piled in the drawer made a nice resting place for them.

It was a long night at the Dove house, partly because Juliet's father was in a state of high fuss about the poetry jam, which was scheduled to take place the next day.

"Calm down, Jack," said Mrs. Dove, several times. "You've never been this nervous before."

"I've never had the head of the college coming to the festival before!" replied Mr. Dove. "They're including it in my job evaluation."

"You created this event to have fun," pointed out Mrs. Dove.

"That was before I knew it could have a significant impact on my career. Drat! There goes the phone again. If it's another of those boys calling for Juliet, I'll...I'll..."

He broke off, uncertain of what to say.

"I'll get it," said Margaret.

She picked up the phone, listened for a second, then said, "Sorry, we sent Juliet to live with her aunt Matilda in Tasmania. You'll have to send her a letter.

You can find her address on her Web site: www.love-magnet.com." Then she slammed down the receiver. "What the heck is going on with these boys?" she demanded, turning to Juliet.

Unable to explain about the amulet, Juliet just shook her head.

It wouldn't have been so bad if they could simply have turned off the phone. But Mr. Dove was expecting important calls from several of the people who were helping him with the poetry jam, so he had to answer the phone every time it rang.

His exasperation grew as the night went on.

Finally, Juliet fled to her room. She was hoping for a little calm. But what she found when she went through the door was vastly worse than what she had left behind her.

Uproar

Standing next to the window was Eris. Though the very sight of the goddess made Juliet want to turn and flee, her legs felt as if they were frozen. Unable to move she simply gasped, "How did you get in here?"

A cold smile split Eris's sharp features. "Have you not yet learned that I am a goddess?"

"You're not the only goddess I've met," said Juliet, startled by that fact even as she said it—and also startled that she had the nerve to say it. "But the others weren't able to go wherever they wanted. It was hard work for Athena just to show up here in . . ."

She faltered, unsure of how to express the thought.

Here in the mortal realm, prompted Cupid, speaking in her mind. *And don't tell Eris you can talk to me!* he added urgently.

"Here in the mortal realm," said Juliet aloud.

Eris's lip curled in a sneer. "That's because the

others are fools and weaklings. They agreed to bind themselves away from the world of men and now have to struggle to return to it. I made no such foolish vow. I have always been with you, and always will be. I am strong—and getting stronger—and will grow stronger still, as I turn the power of the awakened amulet to my designs."

"Have you come to take it back?" asked Juliet, putting her hand to her neck. Though she longed to be rid of it, she did not want to put Cupid in Eris's grip.

She need not have worried. The goddess's response was immediate. "No! The amulet must stay with you. It may not be worn by a goddess. Only the human touch activates its spell."

"If you don't want it, then why are you here?"

"To warn you not to interfere with my plans for the amulet—or my plans for you."

Juliet felt a cold chill. "For me?"

Again the smile. "I am going to make you a star, Juliet Dove, an international celebrity. You will be irresistible as long as you wear that amulet—and you are going to be wearing it for a very long time. Before you are grown, you will be the greatest source of discord this weary old world has seen in many, many centuries. Men will risk all they have for the merest glance from you."

"But I don't want—"

"What you want has nothing to do with it! You are the tool that was sent to me. I am here now just to warn you: Do not try to interfere with my plans—which start tomorrow." Eris paused and looked at Juliet intently, as if she were studying her. "You say nothing. Even so, I sense rebellion in you. So hear this, and hear it well: If you try to thwart me, I will destroy your family. Never forget that I am the goddess of discord. Strife is my art form. I have a thousand, thousand tiny ways to drive a wedge between two humans. You think your father and mother love each other? Let's see what happens after the hundredth argument about who misplaced the keys, or left the top off the toothpaste, or didn't put the milk back in the refrigerator. Those are just the seeds, of course. From such moments, properly nourished, I can raise a crop of bitter, blistering anger that no love can survive."

Her eyes glittered eagerly. "I know the ways of humans, Juliet Dove, and I know how to twist them to my ends. So do not balk me, child, but prepare to walk a thorny path at my side. You will be at that poetry jam tomorrow, or you will pay a price in discord that will wrench your family to pieces."

Juliet stared at Eris in horror. The goddess glared back, her gaze filled with cold contempt. "Do as I say!" she hissed. "And speak of this to no one!"

Then she vanished, leaving only a slightly sour smell behind to indicate she had been there at all.

Juliet stood without moving, except for the trembling that shook her body, until Cupid whispered in her mind, *Is she gone?*

Yes, replied Juliet. Then, surprised, she asked, *Can't you tell?*

No. Unless the amulet is open, I can't see what's going on around you. I can only hear it.

Juliet opened the amulet. But before she could say anything else to Cupid, Jerome poked his head out of the drawer where he and Roxanne had been hidden. "Whoa!" he said. "That is one nasty goddess!"

"What am I going to do?" wailed Juliet.

"I dunno," said Roxanne, poking her head up beside Jerome. "Normally we'd just go get Mr. Elives. Only—"

"Only he ain't there," said Jerome. "So we're on our own!"

Juliet felt another swell of panic. "What am I going to do tomorrow? I don't want to be part of her crazy scheme!"

"We have to think," said Cupid, speaking aloud.

Which they did.

After a while Juliet went to get Byron, figuring they could use all the help they could get.

By midnight they had their plan.

"Do you think this will really work?" asked Juliet.

"Who knows?" said Jerome. "But it's better than nothing."

Juliet had to agree.

Even so, she did not sleep much that night.

Valentine's Day in Venus Harbor dawned clear and bright. Mrs. Dove had agreed to provide a special breakfast for the judges and other people who were helping at the poetry jam, so she left the house early, extracting a promise from the children to meet her at the school no later than nine o'clock. Mr. Dove had gone over even earlier.

Margaret gathered them all together. "What's that?" she asked, pointing to the cardboard box that Juliet was carrying.

"It's a surprise," said Juliet, blushing a little. "I'm bringing it for Dad." She felt comfortable saying this since, while she had no intention of giving what was in the box to her father, she was indeed doing this at least in part for him.

Margaret scowled at her. "Look, Juliet, do you know what's really going on here?"

Juliet felt a surge of hope. Was it possible Margaret knew about the amulet? No, that couldn't be. But what was her sister talking about, then? Mutely, Juliet shook her head.

"All right, listen, you three. Dad's job is on the line today. They've got a money problem at the college, and they're cutting people right and left. Three people in his department have to go, and he might be one of them. A couple of big shots are coming to evaluate the festival and it's going to be a big part of how they decide whether to keep him or not."

"Mr. Toe doesn't like this!" cried Clarice.

"Like it or not, you three need to know about it. If Dad gets fired, we might have to move."

"You mean leave Venus Harbor?" gasped Juliet.

"That's exactly what I mean."

"I don't get it," said Byron. "Mom makes enough money from her comic strip to support the family. Why would we have to move?"

Margaret shook her head. "Mom and Dad may think they're liberated, but Dad isn't the kind of guy who can let his wife support him. Besides, he's got to teach; it's in his blood. So if he loses his job here, he'll start looking for one somewhere else. Now come on, let's go. But don't forget what I said. And don't do anything to screw this up!"

Juliet swallowed hard. Given the fact that she was a walking love bomb, probably the smartest thing to do would be to skip the poetry jam altogether. But if she did that, Eris would turn the full force of her wrath on the family and try to tear them apart.

She felt as if she were being torn apart herself.

It was 8:15 when the Dove children left their house.

By 8:20, approximately three dozen boys were following them down the sidewalk.

"This is ridiculous!" cried Margaret. "What is going on here?"

"Juliet's irresistible," said Byron, sounding very amused.

Margaret stared at her siblings suspiciously.

"And she's got rats," said Clarice. "Only, you can't see them anymore because they've been invisible ever since they got their wings."

Given Clarice's long history with Mr. Toe, this comment raised no suspicion at all.

"Wow!" said Byron, as their parade—now nearly fifty strong since more boys had joined them along the way—reached the high school parking lot.

"Look at all the TV vans. Dad's going to be in media heaven!"

Indeed, four vans from various television stations were parked in the driveway, including one from a national news network. Another van, bigger than the others, had the words SCOTT WILLIS, THE RHYMING WEATHERMAN painted on the side. Parked behind it was a black limousine that Juliet was pretty sure had been used to bring in Corey Falcon.

Ten or twelve people were parading up and down with signs protesting the celebrity guests. "Weather or not, you're no poet!" said one. "Actors should stick to acting!" said another.

This is part of Eris's plan, isn't it? Juliet thought to Cupid. *She wants to create an uproar and have it broadcast on national television.*

That's part of it, replied Cupid. *But the bigger part is to make sure that you get seen.*

WHAT?

She wants to make you a star, Juliet. This is step one.

Juliet would have turned and bolted had it not been for Eris's threat of the night before. Fear battled fear, until her terror over the damage the goddess of discord might wreak on her family forced her to push aside her shyness.

They hurried into the school, where they found a crowd of people trying to register for the day's events. Two coffee stations had been set up, and high school kids were acting as guides for the numerous out-of-towners. Large posters announced the schedule, which started with a major reading by the guest poets in the main auditorium.

"See you guys later," said Margaret. "I've got to go help Mom. Don't forget what I told you!"

"We won't," promised Byron.

Juliet said nothing, for she had just spotted Eris. The goddess had her hair pulled back in a tight bun. She was wearing the same outfit she had had on the day Juliet entered the shop, except that over it she had a flowing red cape. Oddly, she didn't look out of place here in the gathering of poets, many of whom were flamboyantly dressed. Eris's name tag, inscribed in bold letters that Juliet could see from twenty feet away, said "Cris DiSorde."

Eris looked at Juliet and smiled. She reminded Juliet of a shark.

People began to file into the auditorium. "Come on," said Byron. "Let's go find Dad."

Juliet was afraid Eris would follow them, but the goddess went into the auditorium with the poets and poetry fans. The three Dove children went down the long hall that led to the back of the auditorium, where they were to meet their father. They were startled to find guards at the door, but fortunately they had their special passes.

"Let's see what's in the box, kid," said one of the guards.

Byron held it up to him. "T-shirts," he said, "for some of the poets."

The guard opened it, looked inside, and said, "Would have been nice if you could have bought some new ones. Okay, go on in."

They found Mr. Dove standing with Scott Willis, who was even balder and chunkier than he looked on

TV; and Corey Falcon, who was even more handsome than he seemed in the movies.

"Ah, here you are!" cried Mr. Dove. "I want you to meet our guests."

"Well, well," said Corey Falcon, flashing her a dazzling smile. "What a stunning young lady!"

"Stand aside, youngster!" said Scott Willis. "I saw her first!"

Corey Falcon doubled his hand into a fist, and for a moment Juliet feared he was going to punch Scott Willis.

"Almost ready to start!" said Mr. Dove, stepping quickly between the two men. He looked at Juliet and frowned.

As if it were my fault! she thought indignantly, stepping away from the adults.

"Looks like the amulet's effects are getting worse and worse," whispered Byron.

Juliet nodded gloomily.

The buzzing from the auditorium was growing louder.

"Time to get started!" said Mr. Dove, clearly happy and nervous at the same time. "Wish me luck, kids!"

"Good luck, Dad," said Juliet and Byron. Clarice rushed over and kissed his hand seven times.

Mr. Dove walked onto the stage and took his place at the podium. There was a smattering of applause, after which he said, "Welcome, everyone, to Venus Harbor's third annual Valentine's Day Poetry Jam, an extravaganza of words for lovers—and love for words."

Then he read a long list—too long, Juliet thought—of people who had helped make the event possible. When that was done, he cried, "And here to kick off the festivities is America's favorite rhyming weatherman, Scott Willis!"

The audience applauded, but not as vigorously as Juliet would have expected. She peeked out from behind the curtain. A lot of people looked very happy. But many others were scowling.

Scott Willis went to the podium and began to read in a bouncy, singsongy voice.

"Welcome, all, to Venus Harbor
  And the festival of verse,
  Where poems float both port and starboard
  And prose is but a curse."

"That's not poetry!" cried a sharp voice. "It's doggerel!"

Juliet knew the voice at once. It was Eris.

"Shame!" continued Eris. "Shame for calling that drivel poetry!"

This is not good, said Cupid, speaking into Juliet's mind.

What do you mean? she thought back. *I know it's rude, but she's mostly making herself look like a fool.*

Do not forget who she is. In her presence hidden discontents surge to the surface. Resentments that might be kept quiet will burst forth. She sows disharmony, and harvests a crop of anger.

As if to prove Cupid's point, someone shouted, "This garbage is an insult to true poets everywhere."

"Sit down and shut up!" bellowed a new voice. "I want to hear Scott!"

"Then go watch him on TV!" called a third poet.

More people began to shout, some in favor of Scott Willis, others urging him to leave the stage and break his pencils forever.

Juliet peeked out around the curtain again. It took her a moment, but she finally spotted Eris near the back of the auditorium, waving her hands as if casting a spell. A harsh delight twisted her face.

"Is this jam about poetry, or is it about celebrities?" cried someone.

"If you don't like it, get out of town," shouted an older man, springing to his feet.

Soon dozens of people were standing, most of them shouting and shaking their fists.

Scott Willis, still at the podium, stared at the audience in disbelief. Watching him, Juliet had a flashback to the festival's first year when she was supposed to recite a poem as part of the junior-division competition. She had walked onto the stage, looked at the audience, and completely frozen. Her mouth became dust dry; her face burned red; and she felt such a tightness in her chest, she could scarcely breathe. It was a terror unlike any she had ever known. After what seemed like years—though in truth was only a few seconds—she turned and ran into the wings, her heart pounding. She could still hear the laughter that had followed her.

What had made the experience especially galling was that everyone assumed she had forgotten her poem, which was not the case at all. She could recite it perfectly. It was terror, not failure of memory, that had driven her from the stage.

Remembering all that, Juliet wished she could help Mr. Willis, who seemed like a nice enough man, even though he was a terrible poet. Then she saw Corey Falcon bound onto the stage and felt a wave of relief. Surely the handsome young star would help calm the audience. But to her horror, she heard him shout, "The people are right, old man! This drivel of yours is an insult to true poetry."

"You think your adolescent scribbling is any better, pretty boy?" snarled the weatherman. "You would have never published a word if you weren't a movie star."

"Weatherman!" shouted Corey Falcon, as if it were the worst of all possible insults.

"Movie star!" screamed Scott Willis, giving him a shove.

The audience erupted. Shouts and insults flew back and forth, and it looked as if fists would soon be flying as well. The cameramen from the news channels were racing up and down the aisles, thrusting their lenses at red-faced, angry people—which only made most of them angrier.

Juliet turned to look at her father. His face had gone white, and he looked as if he were about to be sick.

"Juliet, you've got to do something!" said Byron.

Suddenly her fury was greater than her shyness. This was all Eris's fault, and Juliet wasn't going to let the goddess get away with it. In a blaze of anger, she strode onto the stage, pushed herself between the movie star and the weatherman, grabbed the microphone, and roared, "For heaven's sake, sit down and shut up! All of you!"

FIFTEEN

Downfall

To Juliet's amazement, the audience did exactly as she had ordered. A deep hush fell over the auditorium, as if she had just cast a spell of her own.

What happened? she thought to Cupid.

I think an entire roomful of people just fell in love with you.

Juliet's momentary relief was replaced by a surge of terror. Now what should she do? Hundreds of eager eyes that seconds ago were blind with anger now stared expectantly up at her. Hundreds of eager ears waited to hear what she would say next. She stood frozen once again, remembering her terror of two years before. Her throat was a desert, her hands a pair of leaves in a windstorm. Heat radiated from her cheeks, and she wanted nothing more than to flee back into the darkness.

Say something! urged Cupid.

What? thought Juliet, clutching the podium as if it were a life preserver in a storm-tossed sea.

It's a poetry jam, isn't it? Well, let's give them some poetry!

I don't know any poem that's right for this, she thought, still not daring to look out at the audience.

Then we'll make one up.

Right now? thought Juliet, her terror deeper than ever.

Didn't you ever hear of inspiration? The breath of the gods moving through you to lift you to artistic glory? Well, look who you've got to provide it. I'll be your muse. Now let's go!

Juliet smiled at the idea and raised her eyes. The audience was still staring at her—held, she was sure, by the power of the amulet. But to get out of this, she was going to have to give them something more.

Speak from your heart, said a new voice, unexpected, but familiar.

Athena? thought Juliet.

I am with you, mortal child, said the goddess.

As am I, said the voice of Hera.

We will help with the shaping, said Cupid. *But the words, the ideas, must come from you.*

Juliet gazed out at the audience. *What do I want to tell them?* she thought.

From that question came the first words, which bubbled up within her as if flowing from some secret fountain.

"What Do You Love?" she asked, making it clear from her voice that this was the title of the poem she was about to recite.

Good, said Cupid.

Juliet took a deep breath, stared for another mo-

ment at the silent audience, then leaned close to the
microphone and let the words wash through her.

"What do you love?
  What holds your heart?
  Is it truth? Justice? Freedom?
  Family? Friends? Home?
  Or is it something smaller—
  A sound, a smell, a word,
  A voice?
  What would you give up for it?
  An eye? An arm? A leg?
  Your life?
  Or would you go further,
  And give it your heart?
  What do you love
  More than breath?
  What do you cherish
  In the most secret corners of your heart?
  What, if taken from you,
  Would leave the deepest hole,
  The hardest hurt?
  What do you love—
  And why?
  Tell me this,
  And you've told me all I need to know—
  For then I'll know your heart
  And how to love you back."

Juliet stopped, astonished at herself.
Where did that come from? she thought.

You, of course, said Cupid.

Juliet took a breath. She was almost dizzy, not only with the effort of facing the audience, nor with the effort of creation, but with something else that had overcome her as she spoke. It was as if in asking the question, "What do you love?" she had been forced to answer it herself. A tidal wave of love had washed through her—love for her family, for her home, for Venus Harbor, for Queen Baboo, for the little details of her life, the flowers in the backyard, the always present smell of the sea air, even the ridiculous sluggarium. And under all that was an even more astonishing idea, one that fairly staggered her.

I love myself, she thought. And with that realization came a feeling of peace and happiness deeper than any she had ever known.

She was pulled from her reverie by a strange sound. Confused at first, it took her a moment to realize it came from the audience, which was applauding. Applauding wildly.

Applauding for her.

Suddenly aware of herself, of how she had exposed herself, Juliet felt an urge to bolt for the safety of the curtains. Remembering her father's training, she caught herself just in time. Taking a breath she looked out at the audience and accepted the applause.

Then she nodded and walked slowly offstage.

Her father was waiting for her with outstretched arms. "Well done!" he cried, sweeping her up in an embrace. "Oh, well done, well done, my darling daughter!" Then he held her so close she could feel the beating of his heart against her cheek.

Ms. Priest approached. She was not as exuberant as Mr. Dove but just as warm in her congratulations. "Not many can or will speak straight from the heart, Juliet," she said softly. "That was well done indeed. Brave, too."

"I don't even know what I said," murmured Juliet. "Was it really all right?"

"You hear the applause, don't you?" asked Ms. Priest, with just a touch of sharpness in her voice. Then she smiled. "I know how you are feeling. It happens to me sometimes when I am telling stories. Something flows through you, and you are speaking more clearly, connecting more directly, than you thought was possible. It's a somewhat fearful blessing, isn't it? And who knows where it comes from? But it doesn't happen unless you are ready and open your heart. You are part of it. Accept the praise, Juliet—accept it, and cherish it. But don't let it go to your head."

Mr. Dove smiled. "Well spoken, Hyacinth. Sometimes I have a moment like that when I am teaching. It's like finding gold. But for this one . . . oh, my sweet and quiet daughter, it was like watching a mouse roar!"

His words sounded like a bell in Juliet's mind. Was it possible that Mr. Suss's poem had been . . . well, poetic? Could *she* be the mouse who had roared?

If so, they were nearly done. She had found the key. She, the mouse, had roared. Now they needed only a mother's touch to finish the spell that would free Cupid from the amulet. She felt almost giddy with relief. It shouldn't be hard to get her mother to hold the amulet for her, especially if she didn't actually try to say anything about it.

She was still thinking this through when her father said, "I'll be right back. I need to take care of things out front."

Juliet smiled as she watched her father return to the podium. As silence settled over the auditorium, he said, "I'd like to thank Scott Willis and Corey Falcon for helping us prove that the passion for words is alive and well. I'd also like to thank my daughter Juliet for the poem she just shared with you. And now I need to ask you to hurry on to the next sessions, so our day doesn't get completely off track!"

As people began to file out of the auditorium, Ms. Priest leaned over to Juliet and said quietly, "Can you meet me behind your house tonight after all are asleep? If so, I'll take you on a little trip. I think you'll find it interesting."

Juliet started to ask what she meant but was interrupted by three reporters who had made their way backstage and wanted to interview her. To her amazement she didn't mind answering their questions, though she got nervous when they wanted her to go back onstage so they could take pictures of her. She remembered what Cupid had said about Eris wanting to make her a star. But she couldn't find a graceful way out of it.

Don't worry, thought Cupid. *I think it's almost over now!*

As Juliet was finishing with the last reporter, her father was called away to deal with Scott Willis and

Corey Falcon, who were having a screaming fight about lawsuits.

What a stupid waste of time, thought Juliet.

Eris found fertile ground in their hearts, agreed Cupid.

Though she knew that Byron and Clarice were waiting for her in the wings, Juliet chose to remain on the stage for a moment. She returned to the podium, wanting to remember what it was like to look out at the audience and not be afraid, to actually enjoy speaking to people. She started to open the amulet, thinking to show the space to Cupid as well, when someone said, "Juliet?"

Turning, she was startled to see Bambi Quilp standing at the edge of the curtain. Juliet frowned. She really didn't want to deal with Bambi's teasing and nasty comments, not now, not when she had just had such a triumph. But to her surprise, what Bambi said was, "I just wanted to tell you how awesome that was."

Juliet blinked at her, too astonished to say anything at first. Then, to gain a little time—and also because she wouldn't feel comfortable until she knew—she said, "Where's Samantha?"

Bambi made a face. "She's out looking for Corey Falcon. She wants him to autograph her forehead."

Juliet smiled.

Bambi smiled back.

Juliet took a deep breath, knowing what she had to do next. "I've been wanting to talk to you," she said. "About the other day."

Bambi's face tightened. "I'm sorry about that."

"*You're* sorry?" Juliet asked, totally confused.

"I shouldn't have teased you about Arturo. I was just trying to make Samantha laugh."

"Why do you hang around with that leech, anyway?" asked Juliet sharply. She was appalled at the tone in her own voice. She wanted to make peace here, not make things worse.

"She's my friend!" snapped Bambi. "She may not be perfect, but at least I can talk to her. Not like you. What makes you think you're all that special? Because you're good with words? That doesn't give you any right to act so snooty to the rest of us!"

Juliet's astonishment turned to fury. She could feel the tightening in her gut that meant Killer was about to emerge. The ferocious words sprang to her mind fully formed, without her even having to look for them: *You brainless blond bimbette, you wouldn't know a word from a whippoorwill. Why don't you take your room-temperature IQ, go back to your suck-up friend, and leave me alone!*

But then other words returned to her, words uttered by Athena: "Most people know, most of the time, what would be wisest to do. The problem is they choose to act otherwise. Or they lack courage."

Juliet swallowed hard, forcing the poisonous words back to the dark place from which they had come. She took a long, slow breath, and then another one. Then, instead of the angry volley of insults, she said simply, "I'm sorry, Bambi. I don't really think I'm better than anyone. Honest I don't. It's just that I'm very . . . shy."

The last word was barely a whisper.

Something softened in Bambi's face, as if her anger was melting away. She paused for a moment, then asked incredulously, "Do you really expect me to believe *you're* shy?"

Juliet shook her head, astonished that anyone could imagine she was anything *but* shy. "Does everyone think I'm stuck-up?" she asked softly.

Bambi shrugged. "I don't know. A lot of us do."

Juliet sighed. "That's so weird I don't even know what to say."

Bambi shook her head. "Well, if you really are shy, you did pretty good shutting everyone up a few minutes ago."

Juliet smiled. "I had help for that one."

Bambi looked puzzled. But before she could ask what Juliet meant, there was a beeping from her pocket. She took out a cell phone and glanced at it. "It's Samantha," she said with a sigh. "I have to go. I told her I'd meet her. She ... latches on to me. Sometimes it's hard to get away from her. Anyway, all I wanted to say was, I really liked your poem."

"Thanks," said Juliet softly.

Bambi nodded, smiled, and scooted off the stage.

No sooner had she gone than Juliet heard the sound of clapping again. Not from many hands this time, but from just one person. The applause was slow, and if applause could sound sarcastic, this did.

She turned toward the sound. To her horror, Eris was sitting in the front row of the otherwise abandoned auditorium.

"Very touching," said the goddess, her voice

tinged with acid. "Did you stage that little bit of peacemaking just to annoy me?"

"What do you mean?" asked Juliet.

"Oh, don't act stupid. I had you and your little friend all worked up and ready for a nice fight. But you chose to calm things down instead—which I know very well is not your way... *Killer*. Do you really want to defy me, child? The price will be high."

She stood and walked to the edge of the stage. With a single, sharp move—an impossible jump that looked almost as if she had been lifted by invisible strings—she was standing in front of Juliet.

"You've had your fun," she said, her voice cold. "Now it's time we had another little talk."

Juliet stepped back, startled by the intensity of the goddess's wrath. Eris continued toward her, hissing, "I warned you not to cross me!"

Don't worry, said Athena, speaking in Juliet's mind.

She cannot touch you, said Hera. *Have we not given you kisses of protection?*

Eris took a step closer and reached for Juliet. But when her fingers were inches away, the goddess of discord cried out, pulling back as if she had been stung. "So, you have protection, do you?" Raising her head she cried, "Do not think to thwart me, Athena! Save your energy, Hera! Earth is still my realm. Your feeble kisses cannot stand against my power here. If I cannot touch the girl now, I will take her where I *can* teach her a lesson!"

Removing her cape she swirled it around her, clearly about to fling it over Juliet.

"Arturo!" cried Juliet. "Gil! Tyrone! *Help me!*"

Eris looked around in surprise as more than a dozen sixth-grade boys raced onto the stage and surrounded Juliet in a protective circle. Despite her fury the goddess actually laughed. "What good do you think this is going to do?"

"Byron!" cried Juliet. "Open the box!"

Her little brother rushed onstage, still clutching the box he had been carrying that morning. Fumbling with the cardboard, he pulled open the flaps.

Out flew Roxanne and Jerome.

"Fire at will!" cried Juliet.

Eris stared around her, looking confused.

She can't see them! said Cupid triumphantly. *Discord is blind to the messengers of love!*

Eris started forward again, but Arturo thrust himself in front of Juliet. Eris reached out to shove him aside. As she did, Jerome fired a tiny arrow. It struck Eris in the neck. In the same instant, Roxanne, who was fluttering directly above the goddess, strummed her harp. Out poured the music of love.

Eris's face softened and she looked at Arturo with gentle eyes. "What a sweet boy," she murmured, reaching out to stroke his cheek.

Then, as if she had realized what had happened, she shook herself and swung away from him, her face furious. But she was surrounded by a circle of sixth-grade boys, and no matter which direction she started, Jerome was there with another arrow.

She darted toward Gil. Jerome let fly. Roxanne strummed her harp.

Again Eris's face grew soft with love.

"Don't do that!" she cried, as if the experience pained her. She turned toward Tyrone.

Another arrow, more music.

"Stop it!" screamed Eris. *"Stop it!"*

But the Immortal Vermin of Love were merciless. Roxanne, fluttering three feet above the goddess's head, poured out a cascade of music that flowed around Eris like a waterfall of desire. Jerome, fitting new arrows to his bow as fast as he could fire them, moved even closer.

Eris stopped, closed her eyes, put her hands to the side of her head. When she opened her eyes again, they were blazing, fiery red. It was clear she could now see the rats—as could everyone else, since the boys cried out in surprise.

Jerome, confident in his invisibility, had gotten too close. Eris gave him a vicious swat that sent him flying sideways. His bow tumbled from his hand, and the arrow he had been ready to fire fell to the stage. Jerome himself struck the side of the podium. One wing crumpled behind him as he slid to the floor.

Looking up at Roxanne, the goddess pursed her lips and blew. A fierce gust of wind pushed the startled rat up and up, until she vanished in the high, dark area above the curtains.

Eris turned again to Juliet. This time it was Tyrone who stepped forward and thrust himself between them. Eris reached for him.

"Tyrone, run!" cried Juliet. "Run!"

Tyrone ignored her warning and stood his ground. But just as Eris was about to grab him, Jerome—who had dragged himself to the fallen love arrow and then pulled himself across the floor with it clutched in his tiny paw—reached the goddess's foot. With a desperate cry of "Love conquers all!" he jabbed it into Eris's ankle.

Roxanne came down like an arrow herself, plummeting from the dark recesses above, then stretching her tiny wings to stop just above the goddess. Another outpouring of music flowed over Eris.

"Too much!" Eris cried in horror. "Too much love!"

She swirled her cloak around her.

"Jerome!" cried Roxanne, recognizing the gesture. "Get away, get away! She's gonna go!"

But Jerome continued to cling to Eris's ankle, jabbing the goddess with the love arrow.

With a shriek that was equal parts rage and despair, Eris vanished.

When she was gone, so was the rat.

"Jerome!" shouted Roxanne mournfully, hopelessly. "Jerome, come back!"

Silence.

"What will happen to him?" whispered Roxanne, turning to the others.

But for that, neither Juliet nor Cupid had an answer.

SIXTEEN

Love on
the Half Shell

Though they were jubilant over the defeat of Eris, the little group was subdued by the loss of Jerome. Juliet tried asking Hera and Athena if they knew where Eris had gone and could somehow protect the brave little rat, but the goddesses had vanished from her mind.

Gently, Juliet picked up Roxanne and whispered, "We'll find him again, I'm sure of it."

The part about being sure was a lie, but she didn't think it was wrong to say, just then.

Clarice trotted onto the stage and held out her chubby arms. Roxanne leaned toward her, so Juliet passed the rat to her little sister, who cuddled her gently. Juliet wasn't sure, but she thought she could hear Roxanne crying.

"Go back where you were," Juliet told Clarice. "I'll be there in a little while."

Clarice nodded. "Me and Mr. Toe will try to make Roxanne feel better," she said. Then she returned to the wings.

"I'll keep an eye on them," said Byron.

"Thanks, said Juliet, knowing that he made the offer partly so that she could be alone with the boys to thank them.

"You guys are great," she said. "Who knows where I might be now if you hadn't come to save me?" Even as she said it, she realized that wherever Eris would have taken her was probably exactly where Jerome was now. "I wasn't expecting all of you," she continued, "just Arturo and Gil and Tyrone."

"Byron told us that we should be here and ready to move," said Gil. "It sounded like things might get nasty, so we decided some of the other guys ought to be here as well." Then he paused and said, "Juliet, have you been, like, magically making us all goofy?"

"Actually, that was my fault," said Cupid, speaking from the amulet.

Juliet hadn't seen so many boys look that scared all at the same time since the day the principal walked into the room during the Great Fifth-Grade Spitball War.

"This is what's been causing all the problems," she explained, lifting the amulet. "And I'm really sorry, because I know you guys wouldn't have done this without the love spell. I know—"

She stopped, interrupted by their laughter.

"What's so funny?" she demanded.

It was Tyrone's turn to answer. "That spell was broken the minute you roared at the audience to shut up."

"Then why did you help me?" she asked, genuinely confused.

The boys just rolled their eyes.

Oh, Juliet, sighed Cupid. *You still don't understand how much goodwill you generate just by being yourself, do you? The boys helped you because you are you. The audience listened to your poem because it was good!*

We'll talk about it later! she replied sharply, feeling a blush coming on.

They talked for a bit longer, but finally there was nothing left to say, and the boys began to drift away—all except Arturo, who lingered after the others, then said softly, "I didn't need a magic spell to think you're wonderful, Juliet."

Then he blushed and ran off as if Eris herself were after him.

Juliet stood for a while, looking where he had gone and thinking maybe it would not be such a bad thing if Arturo liked her that way after all.

After a moment she went to join Byron and Clarice.

Roxanne was in bad shape.

"Jerome is more than just a friend, isn't he?" asked Juliet gently.

"Of course he is!" wailed Roxanne. "He's an awful pain, but I love the big lug!"

"I will not rest until we find him," vowed Cupid. "He is a rat of uncommon valor!"

"You're not going to find anyone until we get you out of the amulet," said Juliet. "But it shouldn't take long. We've found the key, and . . ."

When she hesitated, Byron said cheerfully, "And the mouse has roared. All that's left is a mother's touch. So let's go get Mom!"

"Not so fast," said Cupid. "We're not sure what's going to happen when the spell is finally broken. Probably best not to do it in front of everyone. Though I long to be free, I think we should wait until we can get your mother alone."

Juliet sighed but agreed that this was probably true.

The chance didn't occur until the day was nearly over. As it was time to go home, Juliet asked Mrs. Dove if she would walk home with her, rather than drive.

Her mother looked a little surprised, then said, "Why yes, dear, I guess so. Margaret can take the car for me."

Tingling with excitement Juliet waited until they were passing the park, which was deserted in the early evening darkness.

"I wanted to show you this amulet," she said, knowing from the very fact that she could say it that Eris's power over her had been broken.

"Where did you get it?" asked Mrs. Dove.

Juliet shrugged. "At one of the little shops in town."

Mrs. Dove reached out and cupped the amulet in her hand.

Nothing happened. Juliet felt her heart sink.

"I don't get it!" she cried later that evening, when she was sitting in her room with Byron, Clarice, and Roxanne. "We've done everything it said in Mr. Suss's poem. Why didn't it free you, Cupid?"

"I only wish I knew," he said glumly.

"Maybe Ms. Priest will have some advice when I see her later tonight," said Juliet.

Roxanne merely sighed.

Finally, Clarice was put to bed. Two hours later, Mrs. Dove insisted that Byron go to his own room and settle in for the night.

The minutes seemed to crawl by. Roxanne huddled in Juliet's lap. Every now and then, her tiny wings would tremble as she stifled a sob.

At last the house was silent.

"Let's go," said Cupid.

With Roxanne fluttering just above her shoulder, Juliet made her way to the first floor. She was not entirely surprised to find Byron waiting by the door.

"I want to come, too," he said firmly.

"I'm not sure Ms. Priest will approve," said Juliet.

"Let him come," said Roxanne, her voice subdued. "He's earned it."

As Juliet opened the front door, she said softly, "I wonder if it makes any difference if we go widdershins."

"Probably not," said Roxanne. "But why take a chance?"

They turned right and headed for the backyard.

Ms. Priest was waiting, just as she had promised. The storyteller was dressed in a white outfit—something between a dress and a robe—and wore a crown of flowers. In her hand she held another crown, which she placed on Juliet's head. "For the Queen of Love," she said, smiling. Turning to Byron, she added, "I'm sorry I don't have at least a laurel wreath for you, young man. I wasn't expecting you. Nevertheless, I'm glad you could join us. You did good work today."

"Hyacinth," said Roxanne. "Do you know if Jerome is all right?"

"I am hoping we will learn what happened to him in just a moment," said the storyteller. Taking Juliet by the hand, she led them to the gap in the hedge. But when they stepped through, they were not in Arturo's backyard.

They were in the magic shop.

"How did that happen?" whispered Juliet.

"The side door is very useful," replied Ms. Priest.

"This is awesome!" said Byron, looking around the shop.

"Greetings, Hyacinth!" cried a voice from beyond the beaded curtain that covered the door behind the counter. "I'll be right there."

A moment later an old man stepped through— the same old man, Juliet realized, that she had seen in the picture Roxanne and Jerome had brought her.

Perched on his shoulder, one wing drooping uselessly to the side, was Jerome.

"There you are, you big galoot!" cried Roxanne. "Where have you been? You just about gave me palpitations!"

"Sorry, Roxie," said Jerome, his voice more gentle than usual. "I—"

"I asked Jerome to stay here with me," interrupted Mr. Elives, his voice more than gruff enough to make up for Jerome's. Ms. Priest scowled at him, and at once his face softened. "I knew we would be seeing you this evening, Roxanne, and Jerome really was not in any shape to travel." The old man paused, then added softly, "And to be truthful, after what I had been through, I was in need of his companionship."

"But what happened?" asked Roxanne.

"You mean after me and Eris disappeared?" asked Jerome.

"Yeah, I mean after you and Eris disappeared! I been worried silly. And *don't* tell me I was silly already, or I'll clout you one!"

Jerome looked very serious. "We showed up back in the magic shop."

"Eris had taken it over," said Mr. Elives, his voice grave. "And I was imprisoned in the back room. She was in a fury over what happened at the poetry jam, so angry she didn't pay attention to little things—"

"Like a rat," said Jerome smugly.

"Like Jerome," acknowledged Mr. Elives. "And, as usual, ignoring little things was a big mistake. Jerome, masterful in his sneakiness, managed to slip into the back room and gnaw through the ropes that bound me."

"The darn things were thick with magic," complained Jerome. "My teeth are still tingling!"

"After that, surprise was on our side."

"Well, surprise and a couple of goddesses," said Jerome.

"Don't get ahead of the story, Jerome," said Mr. Elives sternly.

"Okay, boss. But I wish Juliet and Roxanne could have seen the look on Eris's face when you came charging out of the back room and stopped her in her tracks."

"It was amusing, wasn't it?" said Mr. Elives. "Even so, we might have been hard-pressed to subdue her had Juliet not already made contact with Hera and Athena. Rousing them from their slumber was not the least of the useful things she has done over the last few days."

"Hera and Athena were here?" asked Ms. Priest, sounding surprised.

Mr. Elives smiled, which did interesting things to the creases in his face. "Yes, and they had quite a bit to say to Eris."

"Man, was I glad not to be her," said Jerome. "What a scorching she got!"

"Where is she now?" asked Juliet.

"Athena and Hera have taken her back to the realm of the gods, where she should have been all along," said Mr. Elives. "I suspect it will be some time before we hear from her again." He shook his head. "How lovely it would be if banishing the goddess of discord would end discord on Earth. But it's not likely, alas. One reason Eris found it so hard to leave is that there is so much strife to feed on." He paused for a moment, then said briskly, "But enough of that. We have business yet to do. Follow me."

"Where are we going?" asked Juliet.

"You'll see," said the old man.

He turned and disappeared through the beaded curtain.

Juliet glanced at Hyacinth Priest.

"It's all right. I will be at your side."

Nervously Juliet made her way around the counter.

Parting the strands of beads, she gasped in wonder. What lay beyond the curtain was not a storeroom, as she had imagined.

It was another world.

They were standing about a hundred yards from a moonlit shore. Oddly, it looked exactly like the bay of Venus Harbor. Yet it was utterly different, too, for the houses and stores had vanished and there were flowers everywhere, more flowers than Juliet had ever seen in one place.

"Where are we?" whispered Byron.

"Nowhere," replied Ms. Priest. "Everywhere."

"You always did like that mysterious stuff, didn't you, Hyacinth?" asked Jerome. He had left Mr. Elives' shoulder and was standing at Juliet's feet. She bent and extended an arm. Jerome scrambled up to her shoulder, making her glad she was wearing a sweatshirt.

A strange wind began to blow, warm and sweet smelling, with hints of spice and perfume. The surface of the sea was disturbed now, frothy. She saw dolphins leaping, silvery in the moonlight, and then heard singing.

"Ah," said Ms. Priest. "I was hoping there would be mermaids."

And then she arrived.

Out of the waves, riding on a huge shell, propelled by the winds, came Aphrodite, sometimes known as Venus.

"Wowza," murmured Jerome. "What a dish!"

"Oh, hush!" whispered Roxanne.

It is nearly over, said Cupid, speaking directly into Juliet's mind. *But I do not know the ending.*

Like Athena and Hera, Aphrodite had a high, pale brow. Her waist-length hair was coppery gold and curled around her, seeming to have a life of its own. Though Juliet had seen pictures of Aphrodite rising on a shell from the sea in her mother's art books, in those paintings the goddess had always been naked. Now she wore a gauzy white shift. It was dry, despite her trip across the water.

As Aphrodite stepped from shell to shore, Ms. Priest and Mr. Elives bowed their heads. Juliet followed their example.

The goddess looked around. "It is long since I have stood on these sands," she said. In her voice Juliet heard a thousand bells and other things, too, darker tones, delicious but disturbing.

"Your return is welcomed, lady," said Ms. Priest.

Aphrodite smiled. "Thank you, Hyacinth. This is a strange place, isn't it? Neither on Earth nor in the realm of the gods. A nicely neutral spot." She turned her gaze to Juliet. "I must thank you, child."

Juliet felt a familiar blush creep up her cheeks. "For what?" she whispered.

"I left a story unfinished, and it has troubled my rest ever since. Now, through your efforts, we can bring the tale to its conclusion. Whether it be happy or sad, every love story needs an ending."

She beckoned to Juliet, who did not move at first.

"Better do what she wants," hissed Roxanne, her head close to Juliet's ear. Juliet glanced up at Ms. Priest, who nodded to her.

Juliet stepped forward.

"I know that you have met Athena and Hera," said

Aphrodite. "I am sorry I was the last of us to come through. But there are rules that even goddesses must obey, and since it was my curse that held my son in the amulet, I could not tamper with it. But you have set everything in motion for me to free him. The key has been found. The mouse has roared. Now it is time for a mother's touch to complete the pattern."

"You're the mother in the verse!" cried Juliet, finally understanding the last piece of the puzzle.

"Who else?" asked the goddess. "As it was I who placed my son in this prison, it is I who must free him. But I can only do so because you completed the first steps of the spell, for which I will forever be in your debt."

Aphrodite placed her hand in front of Juliet's chest.

Instantly the chain dissolved and the amulet dropped into the goddess's waiting palm. She kissed it, then flung it into the air, crying, "Open! Open and set my son free!"

The amulet hung for a moment, spinning, spinning, sparkling in the moonlight. Then it began to grow. The singing of the mermaids came more clear across the waves. Soon the carved front of the amulet was taller than Juliet, and for the first time she saw it for what it truly was: a door.

The amulet, which had to be at least nine feet high now, settled to the sand.

Juliet held her breath, waiting.

The carved door opened. Out stepped Cupid, passing easily through the space that once could barely accommodate his finger. He was as Roxanne had first described him, incredibly handsome with large eyes, thick curly hair, and high-arching white wings.

"I didn't know you would be so beautiful," whispered Juliet, finding it hard to breathe.

"It's not necessarily a gift," replied Cupid. He pulled a hood over his head.

Somehow having his face hidden took some of the pressure off Juliet's heart, which had been feeling as if it were being squeezed.

"Oh, drat!" said Jerome.

Juliet turned her head and saw that his wings had vanished. She looked toward Roxanne, who was on her other shoulder. She, too, was wingless. Clearly, Cupid's power was flowing back to him.

"Oh, well," said Roxanne. "Easy come, easy go." Then, dropping her voice to a whisper, she said, "Look."

Juliet turned where Roxanne was pointing. To her amazement Aphrodite had dropped to her knees in front of Cupid. Taking his hand, she whispered, "My dearest son, can you ever forgive me?"

Cupid raised his mother to her feet. But rather than answer her question, he posed another: "Where is Psyche?"

Aphrodite smiled and waved her hand to the right. They all looked in the direction she was pointing. There, perhaps a hundred yards away, a familiar figure trudged along the beach.

"Psyche," whispered Cupid. Then, in a voice that rang like bronze across the water, he cried the name again. "Psyche! *Psyche!*"

The woman raised her head at the sound, cried

out in joy, and began to run toward them. And as she ran, her rags vanished and were replaced by a shimmering white robe. Her tattered shoes became golden slippers. A crown of flowers appeared atop her head.

"A nice touch, my lady," said Hyacinth Priest softly.

Aphrodite smiled and murmured, "I may not have been the kindest of goddesses, but I was always good at the details."

Cupid was racing toward Psyche now, and he swept her up in his arms. And there, while the dolphins leaped and the mermaids sang, the reunited lovers stood on the moonlit beach, wrapped in each other's arms.

For a time no one spoke, but waited for Cupid and Psyche to stop kissing.

"Gosh," said Byron. "Don't they need to take a breath?"

Eventually the lovers broke apart. Hand in hand they approached the others. As they drew closer, Juliet saw that Psyche was laughing and weeping at the same time. The woman cried out in recognition when she saw Juliet, Roxanne, and Jerome.

"I knew your tale had become entangled with mine!" she said.

Then, on the beach that was neither on Earth nor in the realm of the gods, there was a time of stories, as first Aphrodite, then Cupid, then Psyche told what had happened to them over these last many, many years. And again and again each turned to Juliet, to thank her.

They stayed long into the night, and Juliet thought it would be fine if the night went on forever.

Byron leaned against her, dozing. She struggled to stay awake herself, but the day had been exhausting. Soothed by the waves, lulled by the songs of the mermaids, safe in the company of friends, she fell at last into a deep and dreamless slumber.

When she awoke she was in her own bed.

She looked beside her, but Roxanne and Jerome were gone.

To her surprise she realized that she was going to miss them.

She had grown used to their company.

In fact, she sort of loved them.

Epilogue

On Saturday night the week after Juliet had been crowned Queen of Love, she sat in the attic, rocking. Downstairs her mother and father were hosting a dinner for the people who had helped with the poetry jam. She knew her mother wanted her to be part of it, but right now she needed to be alone for a little while.

As she rocked she stared at "The Field of Gold," which was how she now thought of the painting with the goatboy and his goats. Looking at it made her think of Roxanne and Jerome—which made her acutely aware of how much she missed the two rats, if not the chaos that had come with them.

After a while she shifted her chair so she could look outside instead. Gazing through the low window at the end of the attic, she could see the waning moon shining down on Venus Harbor. The sight of it made her wonder where the goddesses were now.

Her reverie was interrupted by a familiar voice calling from behind her, "Hey, Juliet! How ya doin'?"

"Jerome! Is that you?"

"The one and only," said the rat, scampering around to stand in front of her.

"And me!" added Roxanne, as she joined him.

Juliet felt a moment of worry. "Is anything wrong?"

"Nah, we just came to bring you some news," said Jerome. "And a present!"

"We don't always bring trouble, you know," said Roxanne, sounding slightly offended.

Juliet smiled. "How have you been?"

"Busy," said Jerome. "The old man really keeps us hopping. Sometimes I miss those wings. It'd make things easier if I could fly around."

"They were nothing but a good way for you to get into mischief," said Roxanne tartly. "Anyway, Juliet, the main reason we came by was to tell you that we saw Cupid and Psyche the other day."

"How are they doing?" asked Juliet eagerly.

"Happy as all get-out," said Roxanne.

"To tell you the truth, it got a little sickening to watch 'em," added Jerome. "Too much of that lovey-dovey stuff could make a guy hork up his cheese."

"Honestly, Jerome, sometimes you are so vulgar! Come on, let's give Juliet her present."

"It's from the old man," added Jerome. "He said you earned it. And believe me, he don't say that unless he means it."

"What is it?" asked Juliet.

"Read it for yourself," said Jerome. He unstrapped a tiny scroll from his back, then passed it to her.

Juliet unrolled the paper. There, in Mr. Elives' spidery writing, was an invitation:

To Juliet Dove, Queen of Love—

It is rare for someone to enter my shop and not leave with the item that was intended for them. Yet you did so—and acquitted yourself wonderfully amidst the chaos and discord that followed. In recognition of that, I would like to offer you the chance to visit again, whenever you feel there is something you need that you cannot provide for yourself.

This is a one-time offer, so use it carefully, Juliet Dove.

I shall look forward to seeing you when the time is right.

Sincerely,
S. H. Elives

"I don't understand," Juliet said, after a moment. "What good is this?"

"What do you mean?" asked Roxanne.

"You were the ones who told me I can't get back to the shop. It could be anywhere when I want to use this invitation."

"Ah, that's easy," said Jerome. "You just send a message to me and Roxanne, and we'll come and get you."

"And how am I supposed to do that?"

"You're gonna like this one," said Roxanne proudly. "Open that trunk over there." She was pointing at one of Great Aunt Bessie's old travel trunks.

"Why?"

"Will you just do it?" asked Jerome impatiently.

Juliet crossed to the trunk. She knew it had been

around the world several times; it looked as if it had been kicked all the way on the last trip. A pair of tarnished metal latches, each at least two inches wide, held it closed. They creaked as she unfastened them. The hinges in back creaked even louder as she raised the lid.

Inside, on top of a pile of old clothing and papers, was a beautifully wrapped box. Dangling from the box was a tag that said, "For Juliet Dove."

"How did this get in here?" she asked in amazement.

Roxanne tittered. "You'd think you would have come to expect a *little* magic by now, Juliet. Go on—open the box!"

Juliet carried the box back to her rocking chair and carefully began to undo the wrapping.

"Cripe, you open packages just like a girl," said Jerome.

"She *is* a girl, Jerome! Now be quiet."

Inside the box was the most beautiful shell Juliet had ever seen, its throat deep rose, its whorls so delicate it seemed as if they were made of spun sugar.

"All you have to do is whisper right in there," said Roxanne. "Doesn't make any difference where we are, we'll hear you, and come and get you."

"It might take a little while, 'cause, you know, sometimes we're busy or on assignment," added Jerome.

"But we'll come for you," continued Roxanne, elbowing him in the ribs. "That's a promise. One all-expenses-paid trip to Mr. Elives' magic shop, available on request!"

"I don't want to trouble you," said Juliet.

"Aw, don't worry," said Jerome. "It'll be our pleasure. In fact, we'd love to do it! Come on, Roxie—we got work to do. See you later, Juliet!"

Juliet watched as the rats scurried over the windowsill and into the night. Then she sat down in the rocker, cradling the shell in her lap. She gazed out the window at the moon, wondering what she might find when she returned to the magic shop.

The possibilities were endless.

From below she heard music and laughter.

Smiling, Juliet Dove went downstairs to join the party.